Before Paige realized
leaned forward to bru

When he lifted his hea
face for a moment, and then took her into his arms.

Unable to find her voice, she simply watched as he
lowered his head again to fuse his mouth with hers. It
was as erotic as anything she had ever experienced.
Of course, she had only kissed one other man in her
entire life, and although her late husband's kisses
were pleasant, they hadn't been anything like Cole's.
The feel of his strong body pressed to hers sent
shivers of longing straight up her spine.

The unexpected sensation jolted her back to reality
and had her quickly pulling away from him. Had she
lost her mind? Cole was her late husband's brother
and the last man she should be shivering over.

Cole immediately released her and, muttering a curse,
got up from the swing.

"I'm sorry, Paige. I was way out of line. It won't happen
again."

"It...wasn't entirely...your fault."

* * *

For His Brother's Wife is part of the series
Texas Cattleman's Club: After the Storm—
As a Texas town rebuilds, love heals all wounds...

* * *

If you're on Twitter,
tell us what you think of Harlequin Desire!
#harlequindesire

Dear Reader,

This month I'm happy to be bringing you the seventh and final installment of Texas Cattleman's Club: After the Storm. When Colby Richardson was younger, he had a crush on the prettiest girl at Royal High School, Paige Elliott. But when his twin brother found out about the crush, he set his sights on Paige, and before Cole knew it, his brother and the girl of his dreams were getting married. Ten years later, when the Texas twister came through, his brother was killed, leaving Paige vulnerable and on her own. Feeling that it's his responsibility to step in for his brother and make sure that Paige is going to be all right, Cole discovers the crush he'd had on her in high school has flared anew, and this time it might not be so easy to extinguish.

I hope you enjoy going along for the ride as Cole and Paige work toward finding their happily-ever-after in *For His Brother's Wife*. Sometimes rocky, sometimes filled with unexpected detours, the road to love is never easy. But it's always worth the journey.

And as always, I hope you love reading about Cole and Paige as much as I loved writing their story.

All the best,

Kathie DeNosky

FOR HIS
BROTHER'S WIFE

———

KATHIE DeNOSKY

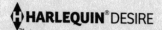
HARLEQUIN® DESIRE

If you purchased this book without a cover you should be aware
that this book is stolen property. It was reported as "unsold and
destroyed" to the publisher, and neither the author nor the
publisher has received any payment for this "stripped book."

Special thanks and acknowledgment are given to Kathie DeNosky
for her contribution to the
Texas Cattleman's Club: After the Storm miniseries.

ISBN-13: 978-0-373-73378-1

Recycling programs
for this product may
not exist in your area.

For His Brother's Wife

Copyright © 2015 by Harlequin Books S.A.

All rights reserved. Except for use in any review, the reproduction or
utilization of this work in whole or in part in any form by any electronic,
mechanical or other means, now known or hereinafter invented, including
xerography, photocopying and recording, or in any information storage
or retrieval system, is forbidden without the written permission of the
publisher, Harlequin Enterprises Limited, 225 Duncan Mill Road,
Don Mills, Ontario M3B 3K9, Canada.

This is a work of fiction. Names, characters, places and incidents are
either the product of the author's imagination or are used fictitiously,
and any resemblance to actual persons, living or dead, business
establishments, events or locales is entirely coincidental.

This edition published by arrangement with Harlequin Books S.A.

For questions and comments about the quality of this book,
please contact us at CustomerService@Harlequin.com.

® and TM are trademarks of Harlequin Enterprises Limited or its
corporate affiliates. Trademarks indicated with ® are registered in the
United States Patent and Trademark Office, the Canadian Intellectual
Property Office and in other countries.

www.Harlequin.com

Printed in U.S.A.

Kathie DeNosky lives in her native southern Illinois on the land her family settled in 1839. She writes highly sensual stories with a generous amount of humor. Her books have appeared on the *USA TODAY* bestseller list and received numerous awards, including two National Readers' Choice Awards. Kathie enjoys going to rodeos, traveling to research settings for her books and listening to country music. Readers may contact her by emailing kathie@kathiedenosky.com. They can also visit her website, kathiedenosky.com, or find her on Facebook.

Books by Kathie DeNosky

HARLEQUIN DESIRE

Texas Cattleman's Club: After the Storm

For His Brother's Wife

The Good, The Bad and The Texan

His Marriage to Remember
A Baby Between Friends
Your Ranch...Or Mine?
The Cowboy's Way

Visit the Author Profile page
at Harlequin.com for more titles.

This book is dedicated to the talented authors of the Texas Cattleman's Club: After the Storm series. Ladies, it was a real pleasure working with you and I hope we get to do it again very soon.

One

Colby Richardson—Cole to his friends and family—pushed his wide-brimmed Resistol back on his head and muttered a word he normally reserved for dire circumstances and locker room banter as he stood in the feedlot of the Double R Ranch and surveyed the damage to the outbuildings. His gaze strayed to the empty space where, up until six months ago, the main barn had stood. The debris had been cleared away, but it did little to erase the memory of seeing the barn he and his brother used to play in reduced to a pile of broken boards and splintered beams. The deadly twister that had leveled parts of downtown Royal, Texas, and several other small communities close by had skipped its way across the west Texas landscape, laying waste to everything in its path—including part of his family's ranch.

Glancing over his shoulder at the ranch house, he shook his head as he amended that thought. It didn't belong to his family anymore. When their father passed away a few years back, the ranch had gone to Cole's twin brother, Craig. Now it belonged to Craig's widow, Paige.

He sighed heavily as guilt and regret settled over him. He had always hoped that one day he and his estranged twin would be able to put the anger and resentment aside and, at the very least, establish a semblance of a relationship. After all, they were only thirty-two. There should have been plenty of time for that. But when the tornado tore its way through the area, his brother's time had run out, and with his passing any possibility of reconciliation between them had been brought to an end.

The devastation and loss of property were one thing, but the death of Craig—along with six other souls at the Royal town hall that day—was another. Cole and his business partner, Aaron Nichols, had used their Dallas-based construction company to help rebuild the town and make repairs to damaged property. But there wasn't a damned thing anyone could do to bring back the lives that had been lost. He wished with everything that was in him that there was.

Taking a deep breath, Cole unclipped the cell phone on his belt. He had put off making the repairs to the Double R long enough. The construction crew he had assigned to rebuild the Lone Star Bar and Grill would complete that job by the end of the day and could start on the repairs to the Double R first thing in the morning.

As he relayed the work order to the crew foreman and clipped the phone back onto his belt, he watched his sister-in-law leave the house and start across the yard toward him. A knot the size of his fist twisted his gut. The moment he'd learned about the tornado and Craig's death, he had rushed back to his hometown to do whatever he could to help Royal recover and to help Paige get through making the funeral arrangements for his brother. Right away it had become apparent that he'd have to keep his interaction with her brief and he knew she had to be confused by the strained encounters. But he hadn't anticipated the effect she still had on him.

The first time he'd laid eyes on her in his senior year of high school, Cole had been fascinated with her. Tall and willowy, she moved like a graceful dancer, and as he watched her walk toward him now, he found himself just as captivated as the day they'd first met. The slight breeze played with her long auburn hair and he couldn't help but wonder how the soft wavy strands would feel as he ran his fingers through them.

"I didn't realize you were coming by today, Cole," Paige said, smiling as she walked up to him. She used the name his family called him and it suddenly occurred to him, she was the only family he had left.

Shaking his head to dispel the last traces of his ridiculous introspection, Cole forced himself to concentrate on the reason for his visit to the Double R.

"I've scheduled one of the R&N work crews to start rebuilding your barn and making repairs to the other outbuildings first thing in the morning."

"Have the construction crews you brought with you from Dallas finished all of the work on the other projects first?" she asked. She had been adamant that the repairs the Double R needed could wait until permanent housing for the displaced families who had lost everything during the storm had been taken care of. Her selflessness hadn't surprised him in the least.

He nodded. "Aaron is in charge of overseeing those crews, but he assured me the last of the houses R&N Builders are contracted to rebuild will be finished by the end of the month."

"Good." She shaded her pretty gray eyes from the midafternoon sun with one delicate hand. "Stella and I were talking the other day about how important it is to get the families back into homes of their own and reestablish a sense of permanence and normalcy," she said, referring to Stella Daniels, the town's acting mayor and his business partner's new wife. "Children need that sense of belonging after what they've been through and all they've lost."

Cole detected the compassion in her tone. One of her most compelling and attractive traits had always been her thoughtfulness for others and he realized she hadn't changed much over the years. Paige was still the considerate, caring woman with a mile-wide soft spot for kids she had been in high school. It was a real shame that she hadn't had any children of her own. When she'd married his brother, she'd been pregnant.

Unfortunately, she had miscarried only a few weeks later and, to Cole's knowledge, she'd never become pregnant again. He fleetingly wondered why, but he wasn't about to ask. Cole had never been one to pry and he wasn't about to start now. What had happened between Paige and Craig during their ten-year marriage was their business, not his.

Not knowing much about what little kids needed, Cole nodded. "I guess it's important for them to feel that security."

"I think we all need that," she agreed, smiling sadly. "But especially after the tornado tore up everything familiar to us."

"How are you doing?" he asked, barely resisting the urge to put his arms around her for a comforting hug. It had to be extremely hard for her to lose her husband at such a young age and in such an unexpected way.

"I'm okay," she said, her gaze straying to the distant horizon. "In the past several years, Craig had had to go out of town on business a lot, so I'm used to spending time alone. But I always knew he would eventually be coming back home." Turning to meet his gaze head-on, she added, "It's knowing that won't ever happen and that I'm truly alone in the world that's the most difficult to deal with."

"I know it's been a big adjustment." Cole stated the obvious.

He wasn't sure what kind of business Craig had been involved in that would require a cattle rancher to make frequent trips out of town. But then he didn't know much about his brother's life beyond the fact that he belonged to the Texas Cattleman's Club—the same as Cole and most of their friends. Cole had even convinced Aaron to join the Dallas chapter after they had become friends and gone into business together. The connections they had made through their involvement with the TCC, as well as their reputation for excellence in quality and value, had helped propel R&N Builders to become one of the premier construction companies in the state.

They remained silent for several long moments before Paige glanced toward his truck. "Did you bring your things with you?"

"No, I'll just stay at the Cozy Inn," Cole answered, shrugging. "I have to get up pretty early and I wouldn't want to disturb you."

When he'd returned to Royal six months ago, Paige had offered for him to stay at the ranch while he was in town, but he had declined. He'd told her that it would be easier for him to stay close to the job sites where his construction crews worked. But the real reason he had stayed in Royal instead of at the ranch was due to the attraction he still felt whenever he was around her.

Paige gave him one of those looks that a woman gives a man when she thinks he's being overly obtuse. "Think about it, Cole. I live on a working cattle ranch. I get up before dawn every morning to give the hired hands a list of things I want done for the day."

"Don't you have a foreman to do that?" he asked, frowning.

"I do, but he's still dealing with his injuries from the tornado." She shook her head. "He was in the barn when the storm moved through and it's a miracle he survived. I assured him that he would have a job once he recovered, so I'm taking over for him until he's able to return to work."

"Couldn't you have one of the other men act as foreman until he recovers?" Cole asked.

"I could have, but with Craig gone I need to stay busy," she answered. "Besides, I want to learn more about managing the ranch since I'm going to be running it alone."

"You could always sell out and move into town," he suggested.

She looked directly at him. "I did think about it. But this is my home now and I prefer the country quiet over the sounds of a busy town."

Cole couldn't fault her for that. He had grown up on the ranch and when he'd gone away to college, it had taken him most of his first semester to get used to the noise of a bustling campus. Now, living in Dallas, he spent most of his weekends in a fishing cabin on a nearby lake just to get a little peace and quiet.

"Living in town would be closer to the charities you're involved in," he said, shrugging.

He hadn't discussed anything about her future plans with her since Craig's death. For one thing, he had made sure not to spend too much time with her once it became clear he was still attracted to her. And for another, it really wasn't any of his business what decisions she made or where she lived.

"And staying here at the ranch instead of driving back and forth to the Cozy Inn would be closer for you while your work crew rebuilds my barn and makes the repairs to the outbuildings," she shot back. "You said yourself that you liked to be close to the job sites you're in charge of overseeing. You couldn't get any closer to the job than staying here."

He hadn't expected her to turn the tables on him and use his excuse not to stay at the ranch against him. "I wouldn't want to impose," he hedged.

She shook her head. "That's ridiculous, Cole. This was your home long before it was mine."

Cole didn't want to go into the fact that he really hadn't missed the home he grew up in. He had too many memories of the altercations he had been in with Craig to be overly sentimental about it.

"But it's your home now," he countered.

"And I'm inviting you to stay here," she said, giving him a smile that caused every one of his male senses to go on high alert. "It will give us the chance to catch up."

As he stared at her, Cole realized that he'd run out of plausible excuses. He couldn't tell her the real reason behind his reluctance to stay at the ranch with her. She would probably think he was crazy, and to tell the truth, he really couldn't say she would be all that far off the mark. It was absolutely insane to be so damned attracted to his late brother's wife.

Resigned, he finally nodded. "All right." He turned toward his truck. "I'll bring my things with me tomorrow morning when we start the job."

"Would you like to stay for dinner?" she asked, walking beside him.

"Thanks for the offer, but Stella has a town council meeting and I promised I'd meet Aaron for dinner at the TCC clubhouse to discuss business." He felt guilty when he noticed the disappointment she couldn't quite cover with her smile.

"Okay, then I'll see you tomorrow morning," she said, turning toward the house.

"I'll be here for the next couple of weeks or so," he felt compelled to tell her. Maybe knowing it wouldn't be just a night or two would change her mind about having a houseguest for such an extended period. "Before I leave to go back to Dallas, you'll probably get tired of looking at me over the dinner table."

His words didn't seem to discourage her. If anything, her smile brightened. "I'll plan on making something special for dinner tomorrow evening to welcome you back home."

Cole's guilt at avoiding her the past six months increased tenfold as he watched her walk up the back porch steps to enter the house. He knew Paige had to be lonely. Her parents had both passed several years ago, and with Craig gone, charity work could only go so far to fill in the empty hours of a day. She was obviously anticipating having someone to talk to for a change.

Climbing into his truck, Cole started the engine and drove down the lane to the main road. The next few weeks were going to be a true test of his fortitude. From the time he'd seen her walking down the hall at Royal High School all those years ago, he had wanted nothing more than to make her his girl. But it was too late for that. She had married his brother and, even though he and his twin had never gotten along and hadn't spoken in more than ten years, Cole wasn't about to disrespect Craig's memory or his marriage to Paige.

The following morning when Paige got out of bed, she found that she looked forward to starting her day for the first time in longer than she cared to remember. What she had told Cole yesterday afternoon had been all too true. Craig had been away on business several nights out of each month for their entire marriage, but she had always known he would be returning home. And even though they had stopped sharing the same bed a few years ago due to Craig's restlessness while he slept, she had taken comfort in the fact that she wasn't alone—that he was just down the hall in the master suite. But the finality of his death not only forced her to face the fact that she had been lonely for a very long time, but also made her realize that their marriage had never been what she had wanted it to be.

She sighed as she walked into the bathroom for a quick shower. Maybe their relationship would have been different if circumstances had been less stressful when they'd gotten married and she hadn't lost the baby. But she'd had very little control of the situation. The minute Craig's father had learned she was pregnant, he had insisted that Craig do the right thing and marry her immediately. Her parents had been older and very conservative and the news of their only child being pregnant out of wedlock had broken their hearts. That was why when they urged her to accept Craig's awkwardly worded offer of marriage—she hadn't wanted to disappoint them further and agreed.

Unfortunately, only a few short weeks after she became Craig's wife, she'd lost the baby and had been unable to become pregnant since. She supposed she could have requested they end the marriage and go their separate ways. But she had made a lifetime commitment when she'd recited her wedding vows and she had been determined to be a good wife to Craig, even though they hadn't been in love.

As she finished drying her hair, Paige decided not to dwell on the past. Craig was gone and, although they might not have had the closeness she had always wanted for their marriage, they'd had a comfortable life together and gotten along well. That was more than some couples could say.

She went downstairs to the kitchen and started the coffeemaker. As she looked out the window above the sink, she noticed that Cole's truck was parked close to where the barn used to be. "When he says he gets up early, he means it," she murmured aloud. The pearl-gray light of dawn hadn't fully given way to the rising sun and Cole had already arrived and was ready to start work.

When the coffeemaker finished, she poured two cups of the steaming brew and left the house. She walked down to where Cole stood looking at a set of blueprints. "I thought you might need some of this," she said, handing him one of the cups.

"Thanks." He smiled as he took it from her. "Since most of the jobs I've been in charge of are on the opposite side of Royal, I couldn't see any sense in driving all the way across town and back every morning for coffee at the diner." Taking a sip, he nodded his approval. "This is the best coffee I've had in the past six months."

"Doesn't the Cozy Inn have coffeemakers in their rooms?" she asked.

He grimaced. "They do, but either I've been doing something wrong or they need to find a different brand of coffee packets."

"Well, you'll at least have decent coffee while you're here at the ranch," she said, taking a sip from her own mug.

"About that…" He hesitated. "I'm not sure it would be appropriate for me to stay here."

She frowned. "Why on earth would you say that? There's nothing improper about you staying here. This ranch has been in your family for five generations."

He stared at her for several long moments before he finally nodded. "I guess you have a point."

"I know I do," she stated firmly. "Did you check out of the Cozy Inn?"

"I have to go back into Royal to meet with the crew working on rebuilding the hospital wing that collapsed during the storm." He shrugged. "I'll check out then and bring my things with me."

The sound of a big truck had both of them turning to see a semi pulling a trailer full of lumber coming up the lane, followed closely by three R&N Builders pickup trucks. "It looks like it's time for me to go back to the house and let you all get started on my barn."

Cole handed her his empty cup. "Thanks for the coffee."

His hand brushed hers, and a pleasant tingling sensation zinged up her arm. "I—I'll have your room ready when you get back from town."

As she walked back to the house, she felt Cole's gaze following her as surely as if he'd touched her. Climbing the back porch steps, she entered the kitchen and took a deep breath. Maybe she shouldn't have been so insistent that Cole stay with her on the Double R, she thought as she set his cup on the counter. When she had been in high school, she'd had a huge crush on him. Perhaps it hadn't completely disappeared.

Thinking back, she could have sworn he had been just as smitten with her. But the one time he had asked her out, she'd had to explain that she wasn't allowed to date until she was finished with school. He had assured her that he would ask her out when he came home from college for the summer after she'd graduated. But he had apparently forgotten his promise and stayed at the university to take a couple of summer classes. By the end of summer, Craig had charmed her into going out with him instead and the following spring they had gotten married. The only time she had seen Cole after that had been when his and Craig's father had passed away.

She poured herself another cup of coffee and sank into one of the chairs at the table. The tension between the brothers at the funeral had been palpable and she never had learned why they were at such odds. She'd thought twins, even fraternal ones like Craig and Cole, were supposed to be close and share a bond that defied logic. But the Richardson brothers were as different as night and day. Whereas Craig had been outgoing and filled with restless energy, Cole was quieter and had a calming air about him. And the contrast didn't end with their personalities.

They looked absolutely nothing alike. Cole had beautiful dark green eyes, was a couple of inches over six feet tall and had a muscular build and straight, light brown hair. Shorter by at least three inches, Craig had pale green eyes, wavy, dark blond hair, and had been on the thin side. Both men were extremely handsome but in different ways. Craig's features were classic and he always looked as if he'd stepped right out of the pages of *GQ* magazine. But Cole had that rugged appeal that sent shivers up a woman's spine and had her imagining how it would feel to be in the arms of all that raw masculinity.

Her heart skipped a beat, and she shook her head as she rose to put their coffee cups in the dishwasher. She had no idea where that had come from, but it definitely wasn't something she intended to give further thought. She wasn't looking to find herself in the arms of any man, let alone Cole Richardson. Even though he was nothing like Craig, she had spent ten years with one Richardson brother and that had been enough to last her for quite some time.

Cole waited until the work crew left at the end of the day to move his things from his truck into the Double R ranch house. He wasn't looking forward to the next couple of weeks—especially after his reaction when his hand had brushed Paige's that morning as he'd passed her his empty coffee cup. If just that slight contact could cause his heart to stall and a fine sheen of sweat to bead on his forehead, what kind of hell would he go through being in such close proximity with her day in and day out?

Pulling his luggage from the back section of the club cab, he slowly walked toward the house. He hadn't been in the Double R ranch house in well over ten years and he wasn't entirely sure he wanted to go inside now. The memory of the night he'd left the ranch for good was an ugly one and had resulted in him severing all ties with his twin. They had managed to be civil with each other for their father's funeral a few years ago, but just barely. As soon as the service had ended, he had gone back to Dallas and, although Craig had started emailing him in the year or two before his death, Cole had deleted the messages unread. He hadn't been interested in anything his brother had had to say.

"I've got your room ready for you," Paige said, opening the door as he climbed the porch steps.

"Lead the way." He took a deep, fortifying breath as he stepped across the threshold and hung his black hat on a peg beside the door.

Cole did his best not to notice the slight sway of her hips as she preceded him down the hall to the circular stairs in the foyer, and he concentrated on looking around the house he grew up in. With the exception of some colorful Southwestern art on the walls, the house looked much the same as it always had. One of the terra cotta tiles at the foot of the steps had a hairline crack from the wear and tear of five generations of Richardson boys' roughhousing, and the honey oak banister still had nicks from where he and his brother had tried sliding down the thin rail.

"What's so amusing?" Paige asked as they started up the stairs.

Lost in the memories, he hadn't even realized he was smiling. "I was just thinking about the time I tried sliding down this rail and ended up wearing a cast on my arm for six weeks."

She grinned. "Not such a good idea?"

"Well, it had seemed like it at the time," he said, chuckling. "But I was only ten and quickly found out that it wasn't."

When they reached the second floor she showed him to the room closest to the stairs—his room when he'd lived here. "I hope you don't mind, but I boxed up the things you left behind several years ago and put them in a closet in Craig's…in the office just off the family room."

"You should have just thrown them away," he said, setting his suitcase on the bench at the end of the bed. He was surprised Craig hadn't insisted on her disposing of everything he had left behind. "I really wouldn't have cared."

"I couldn't do that. They weren't mine to get rid of." Shaking her head, she opened the curtains to let the late-afternoon sun brighten the room. "There were several sports trophies and medals. You earned those in high school, and I thought you might eventually want them."

"I'll go through the box while I'm here to see if there's anything I want to keep," he finally said, swallowing hard. Backlit by the sunshine coming through the window, she looked absolutely gorgeous, and if he hadn't already realized the extent of the attraction he still felt for her before, he sure as hell did now. Her dark auburn hair seemed to glow with shades of red and gold and emphasized her flawless peaches-and-cream complexion.

They stared at each other for several seconds before she started toward the door. "I'd better check on dinner. It should be ready in about twenty minutes if you'd like to wash up."

"Yeah, I'll be down as soon as I shower and change clothes."

When she pulled the door shut behind her, Cole took a deep breath, turned to get a clean set of clothes from his luggage and then headed toward the adjoining bathroom. It was going to cost him a fortune in overtime and his work crew was probably going to end up despising him for it, but he was going to push them to get the Double R job finished in record time. His peace of mind depended on it and for a couple of different reasons.

At one time the Double R ranch house had been his home, but there were too many unpleasant memories of the clashes he'd had with his twin for Cole to be comfortable staying there. When they were growing up, he had dismissed Craig's narcissism and need to win as just being overly competitive. But when his brother had involved others—unconcerned if they got hurt in his game of one-upmanship—Cole had quickly realized Craig was driven by a dark side that seemed to be directed exclusively toward him.

As he finished his shower and pulled on a clean shirt and jeans, Cole gritted his teeth when he thought of their last confrontation. Before he'd had a chance to ask Paige out, Craig had somehow figured out the extent of the attraction Cole had for her and it was as if he had thrown down a gauntlet that Craig quickly picked up. When Craig had taunted him with his intentions of bedding her before Cole had the opportunity to ask her out, they had come to blows. Cole had even tried to divert his twin from his mission by telling him that he was no longer interested in Paige. But it hadn't worked and the next thing he knew, Paige was pregnant and she and his brother were getting married.

Taking a deep breath, Cole tried to release the rage that still gripped him whenever he thought of the callous way Craig had used Paige. It was one thing for his twin to come after him, but when his brother had involved her in his vindictive game, Craig had crossed a line. In Cole's opinion, it was unforgivable.

But that was ancient history now. His window of opportunity with her had closed long ago. No matter what lengths Craig had gone to in order to win Paige, Cole had to accept the fact that she had remained with his brother for more than a decade. That had to mean they had been committed to their marriage, and whether or not he and his twin had gotten along, Cole was bound to honor that.

Two

"I hope you like country fried steak," Paige said, looking up when Cole walked into the kitchen.

The faint scent of his woodsy aftershave put her senses on full alert, but it was the way he looked that caused her pulse to race. His short, light brown hair was still damp from his shower, and he'd shaved off his five o'clock shadow. She barely resisted the urge to sigh when her gaze drifted lower. He was wearing a gray T-shirt with the R&N Builders logo in red, white and blue on the front; the knit fabric had to stretch to accommodate his bulging biceps and emphasized his well-developed shoulders and chest muscles. Her gaze traveled farther, causing her pulse to speed up. His worn jeans rode low on his narrow hips and clung to his muscular thighs like a second skin. She had to force herself to concentrate on removing the apple pie from the oven without dropping it.

Why did Cole have to be so good-looking and so darned masculine? And why on earth did *she* have to notice?

"I like just about anything homemade, but country fried steak is a favorite," he answered, seemingly oblivious to her wayward thoughts. "Is there something I can do to help you finish up dinner?"

She shook her head as she placed their dessert on the kitchen island to cool, then reached for the platter of steaks and bowl of garlic and herb mashed potatoes. Carrying them over to the table, she motioned for him to sit down as she placed the dishes beside the garden salad she had prepared earlier. "I have everything ready if you'd like to take a seat."

He remained standing as she poured them both a glass of iced tea, prompting her to ask, "Is there something else you'd like? I think I have a beer or two in the back of the refrigerator if you'd like one of those instead."

He shook his head and stepped behind her chair as she set the pitcher on the table. "Tea is fine. I'm just waiting to pull out your chair for you."

Paige tried to hide her surprise as she sat down. When was the last time a man had been chivalrous toward her? She couldn't remember if Craig had ever shown her those kind of manners. Maybe when they'd first started dating or when they had attended one of the holiday balls at the Texas Cattleman's Club and he'd noticed all of the other men pulling out their wives' chairs for them. But she knew for certain that he had never done it for her when it was just the two of them sitting down for dinner at home.

"Thank you," she murmured as Cole sat across the table from her.

He shook his head. "I'm the one who should be thanking you for making all of this. Everything looks and smells delicious."

"I love to cook but rarely take the time anymore," she said as they filled their plates. "Cooking for just myself isn't as much fun as it is when I'm cooking for others."

"You don't have someone to do the cooking and cleaning?" he asked, taking a bite of his potatoes.

"After your father passed away, Maria stayed on as the cook and housekeeper for a couple of years before she retired," Paige answered, smiling fondly as she remembered the sweet older woman who had helped her early in her marriage and had taken care of the house and helped raise the twins after the boys' mother had died when they were five. "Craig wanted me to hire someone to replace her, but I talked him out of it."

Cole frowned as he took a drink of his iced tea. "Why?"

"I'm not the type to spend a lot of time on the tennis court or golf course," she said, trying not to notice the play of muscles in his forearms as he used his knife and fork to cut into the steak. "And until the tornado came through, my charity work only kept me busy a couple of days a week." She shrugged one shoulder. "I had to have something to do to keep me busy."

She wasn't going to mention that she had hoped to fill her hours taking care of her children. But it didn't appear that she was going to have any. And it was too emotionally painful to think that she might never have a child of her own.

They fell silent for a time before Cole asked, "Do you still paint? If I remember correctly, you used to be a fairly good artist when you were in school."

"I hadn't put a brush to canvas in years," she said, surprised he remembered her love of art. "But I recently started painting again and thought I might turn Craig's den into a studio."

"Isn't that room a little too dark?" Cole asked, frowning. "I thought natural light was better for painting."

"It is," she agreed, smiling. "Craig converted the sitting room off the family room into his office."

"That would be a good place for a studio," Cole said, taking a bite of his steak. "With that wall of windows on the east side, the lighting should be perfect in the mornings."

"I thought so, too." His genuine interest made her smile. It was nice for a change to have a conversation while she ate, instead of dining alone in silence. "Craig gave me your father's den for my office when he converted that room and since I don't need two, I think it's the obvious choice for a studio."

Cole looked thoughtful. "You know, the lighting would be even better if the south wall was all windows, as well."

"I thought about that, but I wasn't sure it was structurally possible," she admitted. "What do you think?"

"It would need to be braced up in the attic since that's a load-bearing wall and a couple of beams added for support where the two walls meet in the corner, but I don't see why it wouldn't work." His smile caused her pulse to flutter. "I'll check it out for you before I head back to Dallas and let you know for sure just what would need to be done."

"I'd really appreciate that," she said, excited at the possibility of having an artist's studio with the perfect amount of natural lighting.

When she rose to cut them each a slice of apple pie, Cole carried their empty plates to the sink, rinsed them and placed them in the dishwasher. "No more work than I think it would take to make those changes, if you'd like, I could have my work crew get that done for you before we go back to Dallas."

"Really?" she asked, her excitement for the project rapidly building. Craig hadn't discouraged her love of art, but he had never encouraged it, either. "It could be done that soon?"

"Sure."

Cole's smile made her feel several degrees warmer. How could a man look sexy as sin with nothing more than a smile?

"There's no reason not to go ahead if that's what you want," he continued, seemingly unaware of the effect he was having on her. "The work crew will be here, and even if it takes a couple of extra days, I doubt they'll mind. It will just add to the small fortune Aaron and I have paid them in overtime and travel expenses over the past six months."

"Thank you so much, Cole." Thrilled that she was actually going to have her own art studio, she turned and, without thinking, wrapped her arms around him for a hug.

"No problem," he said as his arms lightly closed around her.

They both froze in place, and to say the moment was awkward would have been an understatement. Aside from the fact that she had embarrassed herself with her impulsiveness, the feel of Cole's solid strength surrounding her caused her knees to wobble. Staring up at him, she could tell that he was just as surprised by the embrace as she was. But it was an awareness in his dark green eyes that shocked her all the way to her core.

"I...um, thank you," she said apologetically, feeling heat color her cheeks. Taking a step back, she hoped he didn't notice her hands trembling as she dished up their dessert. "Would you like a scoop of vanilla ice cream on top of your pie?"

He shook his head. "Not this time. It looks and smells delicious just the way it is." She started to reach for the dessert plates, but he picked them up and carried them to the table for her. "As long as we'll be working on it, are there any other changes you'd like to make to your studio?"

His voice sounded just a bit deeper. Was he feeling the tension between them the same way she was?

"How much trouble would it be to put down a laminate or tile floor?" she asked, feeling a little more comfortable now that they were back on the subject of renovating the ranch house.

"No trouble at all," he said, taking a bite of his pie. He seemed more relaxed, as well. "While we get started on the barn, why don't you think about all the changes you want made and then let me know what you decide later on in the week?"

She smiled. "I'll do that."

As they continued to talk about the renovations to Craig and Cole's childhood home, Paige couldn't help but wonder again what had happened all those years ago. What had caused the twin brothers to have a falling out? And why had Cole left Royal without at least telling her goodbye?

Being an only child, she had no idea about the dynamics of sibling relationships. But she couldn't imagine anything so upsetting that it would make them stop talking to each other for more than a decade.

When they'd first married, she had asked Craig about Cole's departure, but he'd told her it didn't matter and they had never talked about it again. Of course, Craig had rarely discussed anything of importance with her. She had always felt a bit like an outsider within her own marriage.

"Thank you for going to the trouble of making dinner," Cole said, drawing her back to the present. He stood up and carried their empty plates to the sink, rinsed them and put them in the dishwasher along with the dishes from dinner. "It was the best home-cooked meal I've had in a long time." He chuckled. "Actually, it's the only home-cooked meal I've had in years."

"I'm glad you liked it, Cole." She rose to clear the rest of the table, but he was already reaching for their iced tea glasses. "I'm sure you're tired from working on the barn all day. I can take care of cleaning up."

He shook his head as he put their glasses into the dishwasher. "You cooked a great dinner. The least I can do is help with the dishes."

As she watched Cole finish collecting the dishes to load into the dishwasher, she couldn't help but note one more contrast between him and Craig. Her late husband had never voluntarily helped her with anything around the house and she'd gotten the distinct impression that he considered anything domestic to be "woman's work" and beneath him.

"If you don't mind, I think I'm going to call it a night," Cole said as she finished wiping off the kitchen island. "The crew will be here around dawn."

"How many men will there be?" she asked, turning out the light as they left the kitchen.

"Seven, counting me. Why?"

"Tell them not to worry about bringing their lunch after tomorrow," she said as they walked down the hall toward the stairs. "I'll have something ready for them every day they work until the job is finished."

"That's very generous of you." Cole placed his hand on the small of her back to guide her as they started up the steps. "But you don't have to do that."

"I know I don't." She barely managed a smile. "I want to do it." His hand at her back was only meant to steady her. But the heat from his wide palm seemed to sear her skin through her clothing and made it difficult to draw her next breath.

"We'll appreciate it," he said when they reached the top of the stairs. "But don't go to any extra trouble."

Stepping away from him at the door to his room, she nodded. "I'll be sure to keep it simple."

They stared at each other a few moments longer before Cole opened his bedroom door. "I'll try to be quiet in case you want to sleep in tomorrow morning."

"Sleep well," she said as she turned to enter her room across the hall.

Closing the door, Paige leaned back against it and took a deep breath. Why did she feel as if she was still that starry-eyed sophomore girl talking to the cutest senior boy in Royal High School whenever she was around Cole? And why had he broken his promise to ask her out when she graduated?

She shook her head at her own foolishness as she pushed away from the door and got ready for bed. She might have had a huge crush on him when she was younger, but that was ancient history. He had made his choice not to ask her out. Besides, some questions in life were just better left unanswered.

The following afternoon, Cole kept a close eye on the clouds in the Southwestern sky. They had been gathering since right after lunch, and unless he missed his guess, they were in for one of the legendary Texas gully washers. Hopefully the rain would hold off until they finished framing the barn, but he wasn't going to bet money on it. There was more than a fair chance he'd lose.

Twenty minutes later, the first crack of thunder rumbled overhead and he knew their workday had come to an end. He motioned for his men working on the rafters to climb down the ladders.

"Go ahead and start putting away the tools," he said when they were all safely on the ground. "We're going to call it a day. There's no sense in risking one of you being struck by lightning."

"See you in the mornin', boss," they all called as they hurriedly loaded their tools into the company trucks.

When fat raindrops began to fall, raising tiny puffs of west Texas dust as they hit the bare ground, Cole grabbed the blueprints for the barn from the tailgate of his truck, threw them into the front seat to keep them from getting ruined and slammed the door. Waving to his men as they drove away, he jogged across the ranch yard to the back porch. He'd no sooner sprinted up the steps than the sky seemed to open up and pour.

Staring at the curtain of rain just beyond the shelter of the porch roof, he clenched his jaw so tight he could've cracked a couple of teeth as he struggled to keep from cussing a blue streak. It was only mid-afternoon, and just the thought of being confined to the house for the rest of the day and night with Paige had him tied up into a tight knot. How the hell was he supposed to do what was honorable and right when it seemed the universe was throwing every obstacle it could in his way?

Considering the attraction he still had for her, he knew beyond a shadow of doubt the hell he was going to go through being alone with her. The urge to take her into his arms had been almost overwhelming, and if he hadn't realized that before, he did after she threw her arms around him for that tight hug last night in the kitchen. He had known it was her excitement over turning his brother's office into an art studio that had caused her impulsiveness, but that did little to prevent his body from feeling as if he'd been treated to the business end of a cattle prod. Then, when they'd walked upstairs together and he had discovered she was sleeping just across the hall from him, he'd lain awake half the night wondering what she wore to bed or if she wore anything at all. The other half had been spent speculating about why she wasn't sleeping in the master suite. Was the thought of lying in bed without Craig beside her more than she could bear?

"Cole, is everything all right?" Paige asked from behind him. "Why don't you come in?"

Turning, he found her standing just inside the open back door. "Everything's fine. I was just watching it rain," he said, knowing that his excuse for not going inside the house sounded pretty lame.

"You might be out here awhile," she advised with a slight smile. "It doesn't look like it's going to let up anytime soon."

Resigned, he took a deep breath and followed her into the house. "That's why I told the work crew to knock off for the rest of the day."

"That was probably a good idea." She walked over

to open the oven door and check on something inside. "I heard on the news this morning that the weather is supposed to be this way for the next week or so."

Why did she have to look so damned good to him? And why was he having such a hard time keeping things in perspective?

His heart thudded against his ribs when her words suddenly sank in. "The rainy season doesn't normally set in for another couple of weeks."

"I guess it's coming early this year." She closed the oven door and shrugged one slender shoulder. "But you know how it is around here in the spring. We'll probably have nice, sunny mornings and a pop-up thunderstorm just about every afternoon or evening."

It was all Cole could do to keep from groaning aloud. Due to the unpredictable Texas weather, this two-week job had every chance of becoming a month-long ordeal. At least for him. His work crew would reap the benefits in travel pay and overtime when the weather did let up. But he was going to face a lot of long hours confined to the house with the most alluring woman he'd ever known. His only consolation was once his men got the roof put on the barn, there was a little work they could do on the inside—rain or shine.

He supposed he could make a trip into town to see how Aaron and his crew were progressing on the hospital wing. Or he might stop by the TCC clubhouse to have a beer with one of his friends. But checking on the hospital rebuild would only take up an afternoon, and he'd never been one to start drinking in the middle of the day. What he needed was another project to keep him and the crew busy for several days—maybe even a week or two.

"We might be able to work around the rain," he said as a plan came to mind.

She looked skeptical. "How?"

"We could work on the barn and outbuildings when the weather permits and on your studio when it's raining," he said, hoping it would reduce the amount of time they'd spend alone.

"That sounds very efficient," she agreed. "Are you sure you don't mind the extra work? You were only supposed to take care of rebuilding the barn and repairing the outbuildings before you go back to Dallas."

He shook his head. "It will probably take a little longer to get the office converted to your studio because we'd only be working inside when we couldn't work outside," he warned. "But it would keep the work crew from being idle when it rains." He wasn't going to mention that part about cutting down on the amount of time he spent alone with her.

"I don't mind it taking longer at all," she said, smiling. "That room already has an outside entrance to the patio so it will be easy access for them, and since it's on the far end of the family room, it won't disrupt the rest of the house."

"Have you given any more thought to what you want done to the room?" he asked, warming to the idea more with each passing second.

"I really haven't had the time," she admitted. "Maybe we could go over some possibilities after dinner."

"Sure," he said, nodding. When she reached for a couple of pot holders on the counter, he stepped forward to take them from her. "Let me lift that out for you."

"Put it on the island," she said, pointing toward the marble top.

He set the cake pans where she indicated. When he turned back around, he found her staring at him. "What?"

"Nothing." She shook her head. "I was just thinking about possibilities for the studio."

Something told him that wasn't the reason, but he wasn't going to press the issue. Some things were just better left as mysteries of the universe.

"If you don't mind, I think I'll go upstairs for a quick shower and some dry clothes," he said, deciding to make a hasty exit before he did something stupid like wrap his arms around her and kiss her senseless.

She smiled as if she might be happy to have him out from underfoot. "Take your time. Dinner won't be ready for another hour."

"When I come back downstairs I'll help you finish up," he offered.

"That would be nice, but don't feel that you have to," she said, sounding a little breathless.

He nodded and, without another word, walked down the hall, climbed the stairs and entered his bedroom. With his pulse hammering in his ears, Cole made a beeline for the shower, stripped off his clothes and stepped beneath the refreshing spray.

As the warm water washed over him, he scrunched

his eyes shut, let his head fall back and tried to come to terms with what he'd just discovered. Staring into Paige's crystalline gray eyes, he had detected the same awareness he was certain was reflected in his own. And if he'd had any doubt about what he'd seen, the breathlessness he had heard in her voice convinced him that she was feeling the same magnetic pull he was.

So what was he supposed to do? How was he supposed to resist that? After all, he was a man with a man's needs, not a hapless eunuch. But giving in to his feelings wasn't an option, either. He and Craig might not have gotten along in life, but Cole was determined not to denigrate his brother's memory by putting the moves on Craig's wife such a short time after his death.

Cole's first and probably best option would be to leave the Double R as fast as he could. But where would he go?

He was certain his room at the Cozy Inn had already been taken. They only had so many, and with the influx of workers there to rebuild the town needing a place to stay, the owners had a waiting list for their rooms, along with every other hotel or motel in the area. And crashing at Aaron Nichols's place was out of the question. Even though he and his wife had just moved into a beautiful new home in one of Royal's exclusive subdivisions, Aaron and Stella were newlyweds. There was no way Cole was going to intrude on their time together.

The only other option he had was to stay on the ranch, hope the weather cooperated enough for him to work his ass off and get the job done as quickly as possible. Then he intended to get back to Dallas as fast as his truck could take him.

Gritting his teeth against the heat building in his lower belly, Cole reached out and turned the warm water into an icy spray. The next couple of weeks stretched out before him like a life sentence, and he was going to have to fight with everything in him to keep from acting on the attraction. But he was determined to do the right thing or die trying.

After a rather silent dinner, Paige poured herself and Cole a cup of coffee. "Would you like to go out on the porch to have our coffee while we talk about my studio?"

"Isn't it a little chilly for that?" he asked as he accepted the mug she handed him.

"I have a jacket," she said, laughing. "Besides, I love listening to the falling rain. It's very calming."

She omitted the fact that she needed the wide-open feel of being outside in the hope of easing some of the tension between them. With Cole in residence, the normally spacious two-story house felt a whole lot smaller and made her more aware than ever of the attraction still simmering between them. She might have been able to ignore it if she hadn't seen the heightened awareness in his eyes that afternoon when he'd helped her remove the cake from the oven. But all it had taken was one look and she knew they were both dancing around on thin ice.

"Here, let me help you with that," he said, setting

his coffee on the counter when she reached for her denim jacket on one of the pegs beside the back door.

When he took her jacket from her, Cole's hand brushed hers, sending a delightful tingle up her arm. "I—I was just going to throw it around me," she stammered.

Nodding, he stepped behind her to gently drape the garment over her shoulders. His hand seemed to linger a little longer than was necessary, and it was all she could do to keep from leaning her head to the side to lay her cheek against the back of it.

"Ready?" he asked, picking up his coffee mug. When she nodded, he reached around her to open the door. "Ladies first."

As they walked out onto the porch and sat down in the swing, Paige realized she'd made a serious error in judgment. She hadn't even considered how intimate it would feel as the sun went down and the dark night enveloped them.

"Besides the floor and another wall of windows, what do you want done to your studio?" he asked, setting the swing into motion.

"Would it be a lot of trouble to add a couple of cabinets for storing paints and canvas?" she asked, happy to focus on something besides the man seated on the other end of the swing.

"It wouldn't be any trouble at all." He took a sip of his coffee. "In fact, we could even add a sink for cleanup if you want."

She liked the idea, but she wasn't sure how difficult

that would be. "Wouldn't that be a lot more work add-ing the extra plumbing?"

Cole shook his head. "Not really. The north wall already has water and drain pipes running inside of it for the half bath on the other side. It's just a matter of tapping into those."

Enthused by the way the plans were shaping up, Paige set her coffee cup on the small wicker table be-side the swing and turned to face him. "That would be fantastic. Since I mostly work with acrylics and water-colors, I'll be able to rinse and clean brushes without having to leave the room and run the risk of dripping paint on something."

"It's nice to see you're excited about it." His smile caused a tiny flutter in the pit of her stomach. "And I'm glad I'm able to help make it happen."

Suddenly self-conscious, Paige laughed nervously as she sat back in the swing to stare down at her hands. "I'm sorry. You probably think it's silly for a grown woman to be this enthusiastic about something as com-monplace as redecorating a room."

He placed one index finger under her chin to lift her head until her gaze met his. "Not at all. Why would you think that?"

"I suppose it's because I've never done something like this before," she admitted. "Craig liked the way the house was and discouraged me whenever I men-tioned wanting to change anything about it."

Cole's only reaction was a slight narrowing of his dark green eyes. "It's your house now, Paige. You can do whatever you want with it." His touch and the gentle tone of his deep voice sent a shiver up her spine and made her more aware than ever that there was still a spark between them.

Before she realized what was happening, Cole leaned forward to brush her lips with his. When he lifted his head, he seemed to search her face for a moment before he set his coffee cup beside hers on the wicker table, then took her into his arms.

Unable to find her voice, she simply watched as he lowered his head again to fuse their mouths. The feel of his lips as he slowly, methodically acquainted himself with hers was as erotic as anything she had ever experienced. Of course, she had only kissed one other man in her entire life, and although her late husband's kisses had been pleasant, they hadn't been anything like Cole's. Warm and pleasantly firm, Cole's lips caressed hers in a way that made her feel as if he was worshipping her.

When he softly traced her mouth with his tongue, then coaxed her to open for him, Paige couldn't have denied him access if her life depended on it. As she parted her lips, her heart beat double time and at his first gentle stroking of her inner recesses, she felt as if she would melt into a puddle. When his arms tightened around her, Paige automatically wrapped hers around him and held on as the feel of his strong body pressed to hers sent shivers of longing straight up her spine.

The unexpected sensation jolted her back to reality and quickly had her pulling away from him. Had she lost her mind? Cole was her late husband's brother and the last man she should be shivering over.

Cole immediately released her and, muttering a curse, got up from the swing. Walking over to the porch rail, he kept his back to her and remained silent.

Unsure of what else to do, she rose to her feet and picked up their coffee cups from the wicker table. "I... um, I'm pretty tired. I think I'll go ahead and turn in for the night."

As she started to open the back door, he finally spoke. "I'm sorry, Paige. I was way out of line. It won't happen again."

"It...wasn't entirely...your fault," she said honestly as she continued into the house.

After placing their cups in the dishwasher, she went straight upstairs to her room. Why did she feel so confused about Cole kissing her?

She had known what he intended to do when he set his coffee cup down and took her into his arms. He'd given her ample time to resist, but she hadn't made a single move to stop him. Why not?

Lowering herself to the side of the bed, she shook her head. She knew exactly why she hadn't protested. The truth of the matter was, she had wanted him to kiss her. And a part of her wished that he hadn't stopped.

Paige took a deep breath. Had she been so lonely that she fell into the arms of the first man who showed her the slightest bit of attention? Or was it the identity of the man that was responsible for her atypical behavior?

She suspected it might just be a combination of both.

Three

After spending a second sleepless night thinking about the woman across the hall, Cole was bone tired and more than a little irritable. Half of the crew was down with food poisoning from grabbing dinner out of a vending machine at a gas station the night before, everything on the build was taking twice as long because of their absence and the weather was threatening to end the workday early again. The only thing that seemed to have gone right the entire morning was his managing to get up and leave the house without running into Paige.

"Larry, watch what the hell you're doing!" Cole shouted as the man barely missed hitting another one of the workers in the head with a board.

When Larry Martin turned to give him a questioning look, Cole immediately noticed his pallor. A ghost couldn't have had less color. "Did you get a sandwich out of that vending machine last night like the others?" Cole asked.

Larry nodded. "We all had the egg salad sandwiches."

"What about you two?" Cole asked, turning to the other men.

"No way, boss." Harold Jenkins grinned. "Me and Terry had better sense."

"Yeah, we went through the drive-through at the Moo & Cackle and got a healthy meal," Terry Goodman chimed in. "We both had the macho man burger, a basket of chili cheese fries and a large chocolate milkshake."

"I'm glad you didn't decide on something unhealthy," Cole said drily.

"I think I'm dying," Larry complained, holding his stomach.

"Go ahead and pack it in for today," Cole said, resigned to the fact that with the majority of his crew out sick there was no way they could get anything else done on the build. "One of you call me in the morning to let me know how many of you are able to work."

While Harold and Terry loaded tools into the truck, Cole rolled up the blueprints. "Larry, I want you and the other three who ate from that vending machine to go to the urgent care clinic at Royal Memorial Hospital," he said, placing the barn plans in the seat of his truck. "R&N Builders will pay for the visit and whatever medication the doctor prescribes."

"Thanks…boss," Larry said, sounding worse by the minute.

"But do me a favor. Don't eat egg salad out of a vending machine again," Cole advised.

"I don't think…I'll ever eat…again," Larry moaned.

If he felt as bad as he looked, Cole couldn't say he blamed the man. "Just get to feeling better. You can worry about what you eat after that."

As he walked toward the house, he watched the R&N truck drive down the lane and felt first one, then another drop of rain land on his forearm. In no time, it was a steady shower and by the time he climbed the back porch steps, the sky opened up with another downpour. It wasn't even lunchtime and the rain had already set in for the day.

Staring at the back door, he wondered what he was going to say to Paige. Would she want to talk about last night? Or would she prefer to act as if the kiss never happened?

He guessed he could come up with some excuse to make the five-mile drive into Royal in order to avoid the situation entirely, but that would only delay the inevitable. Besides, he had never been the kind of man who avoided confrontations. He preferred to hit a problem head-on, deal with it and put the issue behind him.

He opened the door, entered the kitchen and looked around. He had expected to find Paige getting ready to make lunch, but she was nowhere in sight.

"Paige," he called, walking down the hall.

"I'm in Craig's off…in the room I'm turning into

my studio," she called back, correcting herself mid-sentence.

Cole walked across the family room to the door-way of what had been the sitting room when he'd lived there. When he realized Paige was cleaning out his brother's desk, he picked up a filled box. "Where do you want this?" he asked.

"In the den," she said, brushing a wayward strand of her long auburn hair from her cheek. "I wanted to get the room cleared out so your men can get started on the studio whenever they're ready. I can go through Craig's things later."

"I assume Craig had the accounting records and breeding registers on a computer?" he asked, picking up one of the filled boxes. "Do you need that moved, too?"

"Craig used a laptop for everything," she said, open-ing one of the desk drawers to poke around inside. "I moved it into my office the week after his funeral."

Carrying the box to the den, he realized that Paige hadn't yet looked him directly in the eye. He hated that she felt embarrassed or awkward about something that hadn't been her doing. He was the one who'd ini-tiated the kiss, and he was going to take full respon-sibility for it.

"Paige, we need to talk about last night," he stated when he returned to find her sifting through the con-tents of a small tin box.

"I'd rather not," she said, continuing to give her full attention to the container.

He walked over to where she sat in the chair behind the desk and, moving the tin out of the way, took her hands in his to pull her to her feet. "Look at me," Cole commanded when she kept her gaze trained on his chest.

When she raised her gaze, he hated the embarrassment he detected in her dark gray eyes. "What happened last night was not your fault," he assured her. "I take full responsibility for it. I was the one who took advantage of the situation."

She surprised him when she shook her head. "I can't let you do that, Cole. I was just as guilty as you were."

"How do you figure that?" he demanded, frowning.

"Would you have stopped if I'd asked you to or given you the slightest indication that I was uneasy about it?" she asked.

"Absolutely," he said without hesitation. "I've never forced my attention on any woman and never will."

"Exactly my point," she said, nodding. "Don't you get it, Cole? I might have been a bit surprised at first, but I wanted you to kiss me. The only reason I put a halt to things was because I was frightened by that realization." She took a deep breath. "I'm still not sure that I'm comfortable with that little bit of self-discovery, but it's the truth."

He had known they were attracted to each other, but hearing her tell him that she had wanted his kiss sent a wave of heat through him at the speed of light. Cole felt his body begin to tighten and barely managed to keep himself from groaning aloud.

"I don't think my staying here is a good idea," he said, releasing her hands to take a step back.

She stared at him a moment before she shook her head. "That's nonsense. All the hotels and inns in Royal are still full of workers here to rebuild the town. It would be next to impossible to find a place to stay. Besides, we're adults. There might be a lingering attraction between us from when we were younger, but surely we have enough control to be objective about it."

As he stared at her, he had to agree that what she said made sense. They weren't and never had been hormone-crazed teenagers who couldn't keep their hands off each other. Hell, last night was the first time he had even kissed her.

"You're right," he finally said, nodding. "We can handle this."

And maybe if he repeated it to himself enough, he might even start to believe it.

After lunch, Cole checked to see what kind of bracing would be needed in order for his men to turn the south side of the room into a wall of windows for Paige's studio while she continued packing boxes. When he came back downstairs, he carried them into the den for her, and in no time they had Craig's desk and file cabinets completely emptied.

As they worked together to clear the room, Paige began to relax. They both seemed to have put last night behind them and were moving toward building a companionable friendship.

"The only things left to move to the den are a few boxes in the storage closet," Paige finally said, unlocking the door to gaze inside.

"Besides my sports trophies, what else is in there?" Cole asked, looking over her shoulder.

He wasn't touching her. He didn't have to. Just sensing his nearness sent a shiver of excitement sliding up her spine and caused a hitch in her breathing.

Paige gave herself a mental shake. The chemistry between them was nothing more than the remnants of a high school crush. All she had to do was keep that in mind and everything should be fine.

Besides, she wasn't interested in becoming involved with any man right now, let alone her late husband's twin brother. Since Craig's death, she had discovered a strength and independence that she hadn't realized she possessed. She wasn't willing to give that up, even for the man she'd had a crush on since she was sixteen years old.

"Other than your sports memorabilia and some of your father's personal effects, I have no idea what's in here," she answered, doing her best to focus on what Cole had asked her instead of the man himself. "Craig wasn't sentimental and never kept anything that he didn't think he could use or that served a purpose."

"If you don't mind, I would be willing to go through Dad's stuff for you," Cole said. "I don't have anything that belonged to him and, unlike my twin, there are a few things that I'd like to have that belonged to Dad."

"Of course. You can have all of your father's belongings," she said, her heart going out to him. Apparently, whatever had happened all those years ago to cause the two brothers' estrangement had prevented Cole from speaking to Craig about anything he wanted of their father's that hadn't been spelled out in Mr. Richard-son's will. "I have several things that belonged to my parents and each time I look at them I'm reminded of a fond memory."

"Thanks, Paige. I really appreciate it." He gave her a resigned smile. "I'll probably get to go through every-thing as early as tomorrow since I expect the crew to still be out sick." Over lunch, Cole had told her about his workers suffering from food poisoning and that they might not be able to work for the next couple of days.

"Well, when they recover we'll be ready for them to get started on my studio." When she looked inside the boxes on the closet shelves, she frowned. "That's odd."

"What?" he asked.

"Why on earth did Craig keep this closet locked?" she asked, not really expecting Cole to know any more about his brother's reasoning than she did. "Yours and your father's things are all that's in here. I expected important documents or something else that would re-quire a little more security."

"To tell you the truth, I never did understand why Craig did a lot of things," Cole muttered, reaching to lift one of the boxes.

As she watched him carry the carton out of the room, she had to admit that most of the time she hadn't understood her husband, either. She was sure it made sense to Craig, but he never went out of his way to explain what he was thinking, and if she asked, nine times out of ten he would tell her not to worry about it.

Deciding there was no way of knowing how Craig's

mind had worked, she picked up the phone to make arrangements for the thrift shop run by one of the TCC charities to pick up the office furniture. By the time she ended the call, Cole had finished taking the rest of the boxes from the closet to the den.

"Thank you for helping me," she said, smiling as she surveyed the almost empty room.

"You did all the work." He grinned. "All I did was supply the muscle."

Forcing a smile, she nodded. She'd done her best not to notice how the sleeves of his T-shirt stretched over his bulging biceps each time he picked up a box. Most of the time she had failed miserably.

"I hope you don't mind something quick for dinner," she said as they started toward the door. "I didn't realize it was getting so late."

"I'm fine with whatever," he said, following her into the kitchen. "Why don't we have a frozen pizza or sandwiches?"

"Pizza and salad sounds good," she agreed.

Going into the pantry, she removed a thick-crust self-rising pizza from the freezer. When she returned, Cole had already gathered the makings for a salad from the refrigerator and started tearing up lettuce into a couple of bowls.

Paige put the pizza in the oven, then helped Cole finish making the salad. She enjoyed the relaxed camaraderie as they worked side by side to prepare the meal and felt more confident than ever that they would be able to dismiss their attraction and might even become good friends.

Forty-five minutes later, as they cleaned up from dinner, Cole asked, "Are you ready for coffee out on the porch swing?"

Paige closed the dishwasher and turned it on before she looked directly at him. Considering that she still found him extremely tempting, she wasn't entirely certain it would be a good idea to put themselves in the same situation.

"Do you think that's wise?" she asked.

"To tell you the truth, I'm not sure. But I don't want you to stop doing the things you enjoy because of me." His slow smile caused her heart to flutter. "Besides, I gave you my word that nothing else would happen. That hasn't changed, Paige. The only way I'll break that promise is if you ask me to."

She could tell he was completely sincere. But he wasn't the one she was worried about.

"I'll make coffee," she said, determined to prove to herself once and for all that she could control the temptation he represented.

But the more she thought about it, the more Paige realized her apprehension was silly. They had worked together most of the day clearing out Craig's office and nothing had happened. But the real test would be whether they could be together in a more intimate setting without anything happening. Once she was convinced they could do that, then she was certain they would be able to move forward with renewed confidence and build a solid friendship.

When she poured them each a cup of coffee, Cole draped her jacket over her shoulders. His hand didn't linger as it had the night before, and Paige silently chastised herself for feeling a little disappointed. This was the way she wanted it to be between them—companionable without complications.

Once they were seated on the swing, she listened to the rain falling softly on the new spring leaves of the live oak trees surrounding the house and tried to remind herself to relax and enjoy the moment. "I think this is one of the things I love the most about the Double R," she said softly. "It's so peaceful out here."

"It's one of the things about living on a ranch that I miss," Cole agreed, his voice just as hushed. It was as if neither of them wanted to disturb the tranquility of the night. A cow bawled somewhere in one of the pastures, causing him to chuckle. "Even when the silence is broken by a cow calling to her calf or a coyote howling off in the distance, it beats the hell out of listening to the sounds of a city."

Taking a sip of her coffee, she nodded. "When Craig and I first got married and moved to the ranch, I didn't want to live outside of town and really wasn't all that happy about being here. Now I wouldn't want to live anywhere else."

"I wasn't aware that you two didn't have a place of your own before Dad died," Cole commented.

"Craig thought it would be best for me to be here with your dad when he had to go out of town on business." She took another sip from her cup. "Your father's health had already started to decline and I didn't mind staying with him. He treated me like a daughter and I don't know what I would have done without his comforting words when my parents were killed in the car accident."

"I'm sorry you lost your folks in such a tragic way," Cole said softly. "They were good people."

"Thank you," she murmured. "It was a difficult time for me."

Neither spoke for several minutes, and Paige wondered if Cole was upset that she had been there to take care of his father when he hadn't.

"I'm glad you and my dad had a great relationship," he finally said as if he'd read her mind. "He deserved to have someone he loved with him who wasn't a big disappointment to him."

Paige frowned as she turned to face him. "Cole, you were never a disappointment to your father. He used to talk all the time about the things you had accomplished and how proud he was of you."

She wasn't about to mention that his father's praise of him had caused a lot of tension between Mr. Richardson and Craig or that their father hadn't approved of Craig's business trips. There was no sense in focusing on Craig's faults when he wasn't there to defend himself.

"I know that things between you and Craig weren't good and whatever was going on kept you away from Royal," she said tentatively. "But your father seemed to understand and was happy that you had built a good life for yourself up in Dallas."

He gazed at her for several long seconds before he turned to stare off into the darkness. "I did manage to see my dad a few times over the years at the Texas

Cattleman's Club when I had to come down here for a meeting or when he came up to Dallas with a delegation from the Royal chapter. But he never talked to me about R&N Builders. All he wanted to know was if I was ready to come back to Royal where I belonged."

Paige could tell that it bothered Cole, but she wasn't going to ask what had happened between him and Craig to keep him away for so long. If he wanted her to know, he would tell her. Otherwise, it was none of her business.

"I think it's about time to call it a night," Cole said a few minutes later. "If the crew is back on their feet tomorrow, I'll need to be ready to work." He stood up and stretched his arms. "That's if the weather cooperates."

"That's a lot of 'ifs,'" Paige pointed out as she got up from the swing.

When he reached around her to open the back door, his arm brushed her breast, sending a tingling excitement throughout her body. His sharp intake of breath indicated that he'd felt it, too.

The air was suddenly charged with tension, and as they stared at each other, she watched his eyes darken with the same desire that she was certain shone in hers. Thankfully, neither of them commented on the moment as they entered the kitchen and she held out her hand for his cup. She noticed when he gave her the mug, he held it so that she could grip the handle without touching his hand. All things considered, it was a very wise choice.

She set the cups in the sink and walked with him down the hall to the stairs. As they climbed the steps, she could feel the heat from his hand close to her back, but this time he didn't touch her.

Reaching the top step, Paige released the breath she'd been holding as she turned toward her bedroom. "Good night, Cole."

"Sleep well," he said. "I'll see you in the morning."

Paige nodded and, without looking back, went into her room. They had passed the test, and he'd stayed true to his word. He had promised he wouldn't kiss her again unless she asked him to. She hadn't asked him to, even though she had been sorely tempted to do just that.

Sighing, she thought about how she felt now as opposed to the way she had felt as a wide-eyed teenager. At sixteen, her feelings had been those of an innocent, inexperienced girl with a crush on the best-looking boy in school. But now she was looking at Cole through the eyes of a woman, and her feelings were far from chaste.

A shiver slid up her spine as she undressed and pulled on her nightshirt. She and Cole were adults now, with adult desires and needs. And although she knew it was for the best that he hadn't kissed her, she couldn't help but wonder if he felt as let down and disappointed as she did.

Cole stopped gazing up at the ceiling long enough to glance over at the clock on the bedside table. He had gotten into bed more than two hours ago and he was still as wide-awake as when he'd first stretched out.

Punching his pillow, he turned to his side to stare at the closed bedroom door. Why did he have to be

so damned honorable? He had given Paige his word
that nothing was going to happen between them. And
it hadn't. But he was paying a hell of a price for his
nobility.

It had been nothing short of torture helping her
empty Craig's office and not being able to take her in
his arms. The sound of her soft voice, the herbal scent
of her long, auburn hair and just the sight of her moving gracefully around the room had tied him into a knot
the size of a basketball. But as torturous as the day had
been, sitting on the porch swing beside her this evening
and keeping his hands to himself had been pure hell.

Feeling as if he were ready to crawl the walls, he
ground his teeth against the tightening in his lower
body. Maybe he needed to make a trip up to Dallas
this coming weekend and give Sally Ann Denton a
call. Neither he nor Sally Ann were interested in a serious relationship, but they came together from time
to time for a "no-strings-attached" night of relief from
the stress and tension of their day-to-day lives.

But even as the idea came to mind, Cole rejected it
outright. Sally Ann wasn't the woman he wanted. The
woman who created the need burning through him at
the speed of light was sleeping right across the hall.

How had his brother been able to spend one single
night away from Paige? And what in the Sam Hill had
Craig been into that kept him away from the ranch so
often?

Cole clenched his jaw so tight it ached. He wasn't
buying for a minute that his twin had been away on
ranch business. There were the occasional weeklong

stock shows a rancher needed to attend, but those only took place a couple of times a year. And he seriously doubted Craig was going to the smaller, local auctions. For one thing, those wouldn't require an overnight stay. And for another, a ranch the size of the Double R didn't normally buy or sell cattle at those because the smaller sales barns couldn't deal with the volume of livestock from a ranch that big. Besides, the Double R raised nothing but top-quality, purebred Black Angus cattle. They had contracts with processing plants to supply the beef for high-end restaurants and gourmet meat shops across the country. A marketing firm handled that end of the ranching business, so there was absolutely no reason Cole could see for his twin to be away from the ranch so often. At least, not on business.

Surely Craig hadn't been so stupid that he…

A sudden flash of light, followed immediately by what could only be described as the sound of a bomb exploding, shook the house. But it was the sound of shattering glass and Paige's terrified scream that rocked Cole all the way to his core and had him throwing back the covers to jump out of bed. He grabbed his jeans and pulled them on as he raced to jerk open the door.

He had just taken a step out into the hall when Paige ran headlong into his bare chest. His arms automatically closed around her to keep her from falling backward.

"I think lightning hit the house," she cried, wrapping her arms around him as if he were a lifeline.

"Did it break the windows in your room?" he asked, his heart pounding hard against his ribs.

It wasn't something that happened often, but he had heard of lightning coming through windows and striking people inside a house. She was clearly all right, but it was the thought of what might have happened that caused a cold feeling to fill his chest.

"N-no," she said, trembling against him. "It wasn't in my room."

"Stay here while I go check the rest of the bedrooms." He started to take a step back, but she continued to cling to him.

"N-no," she said shakily. "I'm going with you."

"It's going to be all right, sweetheart," he said, tucking her to his side as they started down the dark hall.

Paige was extremely frightened and he could understand why. He'd already been awake when the lightning struck. But to be awakened out of a sound sleep by something that loud had to have been a shock to her system.

As they made their way from one room to another, he opened the doors to a couple of bedrooms before he discovered where the damage had occurred. Apparently lightning had struck one of the trees surrounding the house, sending the top of it crashing through the bedroom's windows.

"There's nothing I can do about it tonight," he said, closing the door. "I'll take care of it tomorrow when I can clear the tree away from the house and see the extent of the damage."

"I think I'll just stay up," she said, walking beside him toward their bedrooms.

"It's barely past midnight," he pointed out. "You

worked hard clearing out the room for your studio, and I'm sure you're worn out. You need to rest."

She shook her head and the feel of her long, silky hair rubbing against his shoulder sent a shaft of longing from the top of his head to the soles of his bare feet. "I won't be able to sleep as long as it continues to storm."

He tried to concentrate on what she had said. "Why not?"

"I was never afraid of storms before," she said, sounding a little embarrassed. "But I was home alone the day the tornado came through and even though it missed the house, the sound of the wind and the way the house shook was terrifying. I've never been through anything like that before and I never want to go through it again."

Her fear was understandable, and he hated that she had been by herself the day the deadly twister caused so much destruction. It was nothing short of a miracle that it hadn't hit the house, and the thought of what might have happened if it had was more than he could bear.

"Where did you take shelter?" he asked, tightening his arm around her shoulders.

"I really wasn't sure where to go until I remembered the tornado drills they made us practice when we were in school. They always had us go into an interior hallway, sit on the floor and cover our heads." She shuddered against him. "I took a throw pillow from the family room couch to cover my head and crouched in the storage closet under the staircase in the foyer."

He nodded. "Other than a basement or storm cellar that was the safest place."

The storm outside thundered loudly, causing her to jump. "I hate being afraid," she said on a soft sob.

Taking his cell phone from the pocket of his jeans, Cole checked the weather app he had installed six months ago after the tornado had torn up the area. Other than thunder and lightning, there wasn't anything severe coming their way. Without a second thought, he steered her toward his bedroom.

"What are you doing?" she asked as they entered the room.

He stopped halfway to the bed to gaze down into her amazing gray eyes and gave her what he hoped was a reassuring smile. "Do you trust me, Paige?"

"Of course," she said without hesitation.

"I'm going to hold you while you sleep," he said, leading her over to the bed.

"I…um, do you think that's a good idea?" she asked, looking doubtful.

"It will be fine," he said. Cole briefly wondered if he had lost the last ounce of sense he possessed. But he would gladly suffer through whatever he had to in order to ease her fears. "I gave you my word this afternoon that nothing is going to happen between us and I meant it. All I'm going to do is hold you and make you feel safe so that you can get some rest."

"What about you?" she asked, looking uncertain. "Will you be able to sleep?"

"Sweetheart, I can sleep through just about anything," he answered.

It wasn't exactly a lie. Normally, after working with one of his construction crews all day, he was out like a light the minute his head hit the pillow. But with Paige in his arms, it was highly unlikely that he would be able to so much as blink an eye.

Thunder rumbled overhead and that seemed to seal the deal for her. "My nerves aren't going to allow me to argue the wisdom of this," she admitted, shaking her head as she got into bed.

Although it was dark in the room, Cole could make out her slender silhouette lying on the king-size mattress and her dark auburn hair spread out across the pristine white pillowcase. He swallowed hard and, taking a deep breath, stretched out beside her to hold her in his arms.

At first she remained stiff, and he knew she was as nervous about the sleeping arrangement as she was about the storm outside. But as she began to relax, he noticed a couple of important details that he had missed before. The fabric of her nightshirt was a lot thinner and the hemline a hell of a lot shorter than he had realized. Of course, his attention had been claimed by easing her fears and assessing the damage from the lightning strike when they were out in the hall. But now?

The last thing on his mind at the moment was a tree breaking a window or her fear of the storm. His focus had narrowed to the enticing woman with very little on lying next to him.

"Thank you, Cole," she said softly. "You probably

think I'm just being a big baby about this, but I really appreciate your consideration."

"We all have things that bother us." He chuckled. "You don't like storms. I'm not a big fan of snakes."

"I don't like those, either," she agreed.

When another clap of thunder interrupted the quiet, she snuggled closer and placed her delicate hand on his bare chest. It was all he could do to keep from groaning aloud.

Yeah, he was just a regular saint, he thought sarcastically. If she only knew how the feel of her soft hand on his skin made the blood in his veins turn to liquid fire or how her lush breasts pressed to his side had him throbbing with need, she would probably kick him out of bed, out of the house and off the Double R Ranch faster than he could slap his own ass with both hands.

Her delightfully warm body was quickly making him harder and hotter than he could ever remember, and he suddenly found it difficult to breathe. He did his best to hold himself away from her, but it was all but impossible when every time it thundered she moved a little closer to him. When she suddenly went perfectly still, he knew beyond a shadow of doubt that she had felt the bulge straining at his fly.

"I don't think this is going to work, Cole," she said, breaking the silence as she started to roll away from him.

"It's all right, Paige." He tightened his arm around her and briefly wondered if he had become a glutton for self-punishment. "I'm a man of my word. I promised that nothing is going to happen unless that's what you want."

"That's the problem," she murmured.

His heart stalled. "What do you mean?"

She was silent for a moment before she finally whispered, "I know it's insane, but I do want something to happen. I want you to kiss me again."

Cole didn't even bother to ask if that was what she really wanted. He didn't have the strength to hold out any longer.

Covering her lips with his, he slowly explored her perfection, then traced the seam of her mouth with his tongue to coax her to open for him. When she did, he once again savored her with all of the reverence she deserved.

He'd kissed a lot of women in his time, but none of them tasted as sweet as the woman in his arms. Cole wasn't going to dwell on what there was about Paige that was different from other women. He wasn't sure he wanted to know.

Unable to stop himself, he moved his hand from her back around to the underside of her breast. Cupping the soft mound, he gently caressed her as he chafed the hardened peak with the pad of his thumb. The thin cotton fabric of her nightshirt became an intolerable barrier, and without thinking he reached for the hem of the garment.

He brought his hand to an abrupt halt when he realized what he was about to do. Paige had asked him for his kiss, not his lust. But when he felt her hand move down his abdomen to the unbuttoned waistband of his jeans, his heart felt like it might jump right out of his chest and it sent a surge of heat straight to his groin. But when she reached for the tab at the top of his fly, he quickly took her hand in his to stop her.

"Paige, sweetheart, it's not that I don't want you touching me. Believe me, I do." He stopped to draw in some much needed air. "But besides the fact that I didn't bother pulling on underwear when that bolt of lightning took down the tree, I don't want us starting something we can't finish."

She kissed his collarbone. "All of my life, I've played it safe, lived by the rules and done what everyone expected of me. If I learned nothing else when that tornado came through it's that life can be over very quickly and unexpectedly. Just once I don't want to hold back and do what others think is appropriate or right. Tonight I want to break the rules and do what I really want to do."

Cole closed his eyes and waged an inner battle with himself. He knew it wasn't wise. Besides the fact that she was his late brother's wife, they were barely reacquainted. But he had wanted her for more years than he cared to count and his nobility only went so far. He had reached its limit and there was no way he could turn back now.

"I can't believe I'm going to say this, Paige," he finally said, forcing himself to ignore the complications making love to her would bring with the morning light. "Let's break a few rules."

Four

As she watched Cole get out of bed to remove his jeans, Paige knew what they were about to do was absolute insanity. But she didn't care. For once in her life she was going to throw caution to the wind and live for the moment. She briefly wondered if she was finally experiencing the rebellious stage that she'd skipped in her teens.

But as Cole tossed his jeans to the side, got back into bed and took her in his arms, she ceased thinking. There would be plenty of time to analyze her decision tomorrow. Tonight she just wanted to get lost in the comfort of his lovemaking and once again feel as if someone cared for her, as if someone needed her.

He immediately placed his mouth over hers and gave her a kiss so filled with passion and need that it took her breath away. As he tenderly explored her with the same thoroughness he had done the first time he'd kissed her, Paige gave herself up to the desire threatening to consume her.

The delicious sensations Cole was creating were electrifying, and she was only vaguely aware when he lifted her nightshirt over her head and tossed it aside. The feel of his calloused palm on her bare breast and the pad of his thumb gently chafing her tight nipple caused her head to spin. She had never experienced anything as amazing as his tender lovemaking.

When he skimmed his hand down her side to her hip, then slipped his fingers inside the elastic waistband of her panties, heat flowed throughout her body and sparks flashed behind her closed eyes. But when he parted her to softly stroke the tiny nub of intense sensations within, she felt as if she would burn to a cinder.

Wanting to explore him as he explored her, she caressed his firm flesh as she moved her hand from his chest down his abdomen and beyond. When she found him, she gently measured his length and girth, and then explored the fullness below. Her reward was a heartfelt groan rumbling up from deep inside him.

The strength of his need for her was overwhelming and the knowledge that she had created that kind of passion in him filled her with a feminine power she'd never experienced before. But when he moved to test her readiness for him, her hands stilled and she gave in to the delightful ache of her own building desire.

"Cole, I...need you," she pleaded.

"And I need you." He paused a moment before he

shook his head. "I don't think we'll be able to do this, Paige. I don't have anything to protect you."

"It doesn't matter," she said, feeling a little sad. "I miscarried over ten years ago, and I haven't been able to become pregnant since. I doubt that I ever will."

"Maybe one day you will," he said hoarsely as he parted her knees with one of his. "But right now, I want you so much, I'm willing to risk it. I'm going to love you now, Paige. Is that what you want?"

"Y-yes. Please…I think I'll go out of…my mind… if you don't," she said, her body burning with the need for him to make them one.

As she stared up at him, Cole took her hand in his and together they guided him to her. Without a word, he slowly moved forward and as he sank himself deep inside her, she realized that she had never felt as complete as she did at that moment.

Lowering his head, he gave her a kiss so tender it brought tears to her eyes as he began a slow rocking against her. His gentle movements and the passion in his kiss were an intoxicating combination and she knew for certain that lovemaking had never been as beautiful or as meaningful as it was at that moment with Cole.

All too soon the building tension inside her took on an urgency that only total fulfillment could relieve. Apparently Cole sensed she was close to finding the release they both sought because he quickened his pace, and in no time, Paige was set free by the waves of pleasure flowing through her. She wrapped her arms around him and held him tightly to her when she felt the surge of his body deep inside hers. A moment later he groaned and gave up his essence with one final thrust.

When he collapsed on top of her, she held him to her and scrunched her eyes shut as reality intruded. Cole was her late husband's brother and she had practically insisted that he make love to her.

Did he think she had used him as a substitute for Craig? That was the furthest thing from the truth, but how could she tell him something like that? She didn't even know how to go about starting that conversation.

She could count on one hand the number of times in the past several years that Craig had made love to her. And even though he had encouraged her to move into another bedroom because of his restlessness during sleep, she suspected the real reason behind his suggestion had been because he'd no longer desired her.

"Are you all right?" Cole asked, levering himself to her side.

"Yes, I'm...fine," she said, feeling unsure of what he might think of her. "Cole...I—"

"If you don't mind, I'm pretty tired," he said slowly, as if he felt as uneasy as she did. "Why don't we talk in the morning?"

Nodding, she started to get out of bed, but he tightened his arms around her and shook his head. "It's still raining and I promised I would hold you so you can get some rest."

"But it isn't storming."

"It might start again," he answered, sounding sleepy.

If the gravity of the situation hadn't already settled in, she might have laughed. But there was nothing funny about what she had done. She had practically insisted that Cole make love to her.

What on earth must he think of her?

Embarrassed by her uncharacteristic behavior, she feared she had destroyed the tentative friendship they had developed over the past week. She just hoped there wouldn't be an awkwardness between them that was so uncomfortable it proved insurmountable.

Around dawn, Cole pretended to be asleep while Paige gathered her clothes and returned to her room. He wasn't exactly being a coward about facing her in the morning light. He just didn't know what he was going to say to her. What could he say?

What he'd done was unforgivable. He had known she was vulnerable and shaken by the lightning strike, and she probably hadn't been thinking clearly. But he had wanted her so badly, he'd lost his perspective and taken advantage of her weakness. Hell, he'd even used her fear of the storm as an excuse to get her to stay in his bed after they'd made love because he hadn't wanted to let her go.

He had known as surely as the sun rose in the east each morning that in the light of day everything would change between them. And it wasn't going to be for the better.

Swinging his legs over the side of the bed, he sat up and buried his face in his hands. After she had drifted off to sleep, he'd lain awake the rest of the night, alternating between feeling guilty and hating himself for his own weakness. He wasn't feeling a lot different this morning.

He had done everything he'd told himself he wouldn't do. In less than a week he had abandoned his vow to respect his brother's memory and marriage, and he'd made love to Craig's wife. He might have even destroyed the tentative friendship he and Paige had started to build.

When his cell phone rang, Cole abandoned his self-loathing to glance at the caller ID. It was one of the members of his work crew.

"What's up, Harold?" he asked, taking the call.

"The rest of the guys are still sick as can be," the man reported. "Do you want me and Terry to come on out there to the ranch and see if there's something the two of us can work on?"

"Yeah, a tree came down and broke a couple of windows during the storm last night," Cole answered. He told Harold what replacement windows and other materials to pick up at the lumberyard to make the necessary repairs. "It shouldn't take more than a few hours to get the job done, then you and Terry can have the remainder of the day off. Maybe the other guys will be back on their feet tomorrow and we can resume work on the barn."

"Sounds good, boss. We'll see you in about an hour," Harold said, ending the call.

Tossing his cell phone back onto the bedside table, Cole got up, grabbed a change of clothes from the dresser and headed for the shower. He wasn't surprised that his men were still out sick, but he certainly wasn't happy about it. Besides the fact that building the barn would take that much longer, he wouldn't have the excuse of working to get him out of the house for a while to figure out how he was going to make all of this right with Paige.

He supposed he could drop by the TCC clubhouse for a few hours and see who was hanging out in the club's sports bar, but that wasn't going to give him the solitude he needed to think. Deciding he couldn't do anything until after his men repaired Paige's windows, Cole finished his shower, got dressed and headed downstairs to see if Paige was even talking to him.

As he entered the kitchen, he couldn't help but breathe a sigh of relief when he found a note by the coffeemaker, telling him that she had gone to the Texas Cattleman's Club for a breakfast meeting of one of her charities. She was going to be away most of the morning, but she had taken the time to see that he had a decent cup of hot coffee. Maybe by the time she returned, he would know what to say to her and how he was going to make it up to her for his weakness.

Three hours later, after clearing away the tree limbs and replacing the broken windows, Cole watched his men drive away and wondered how much longer it would be before Paige returned. He still hadn't figured out how he was going to make things right with her.

He stared at the herd of work horses grazing in the east pasture, and then glanced up at the sky. It wasn't due to start raining until later in the afternoon and there was just something about being on the back of a horse that had always helped him think things through.

Without hesitation, he walked down the porch steps and headed toward the shed, where he'd seen a few saddles that had been salvaged when the barn rubble had been cleared away. Checking to make sure the saddles were intact and any needed repairs had been made, he took one of them, along with a bridle, and headed toward the pasture.

After catching a bay gelding, Cole saddled the horse, mounted up and headed across the north pasture. He didn't have a destination in mind. He just wanted to roam. The Double R had more than a thousand acres, and he knew every inch of it like the back of his hand.

By the time he reached the creek, he had a good idea what he was going to do. He had ridden within a mile of Royal. He was going to continue into town and check to see if there was any chance of getting a room at the Cozy Inn. The way he saw it, removing himself from the ranch was the only solution. He was a guest in Paige's house and he had crossed a line. She might put up a token protest, but she'd probably be happy to see him leave. And if he couldn't find a room, he fully intended to talk to Aaron about overseeing the rest of the Double R build so Cole could head back to Dallas.

He checked his watch. Aaron would be at the TCC, meeting with Gil Addison, the president of the club, to discuss the last of the repairs to some of the clubhouse outbuildings. Maybe he would just skip looking for a room and make the arrangements with Aaron to take over.

Distracted by his dilemma and what he planned to do, Cole failed to notice how close the horse was to the

edge of the creek until it was too late. All the rain over
the past few days had caused the bank to be unstable
and when it gave way under the gelding's weight, Cole
was thrown to the ground as the animal struggled to
regain its footing.

Landing at an odd angle, Cole felt a sickening
crunch in his knee followed immediately by a sear-
ing pain. But like any good rancher, it wasn't until he
saw the horse was upright and walking normally that
he assessed the damage to himself. He hoped that his
knee was only sprained, but as soon as he tried to get to
his feet, he knew it was something a lot more serious.

Unable to stand, he used his cell phone to call Aaron.

"Hey there, Cole. How's the Double R build going?"
Aaron asked cheerfully. Ever since the man had gotten
married he seemed to be in a perpetual good mood.

"It's not," Cole answered, trying to move his leg to a
more comfortable position. He gritted his teeth against
the sharp pain the movement produced. "I need you to
take me to the hospital."

"What happened?" Aaron asked, his voice turning serious.

Explaining the situation, Cole gave Aaron direc-
tions to a road the ranch hands used to haul hay from
one pasture to another. It would bring his friend within
fifty feet of Cole's location.

"You'll see a gate to your left," Cole instructed. "I'm
sitting about fifty feet from that on the creek bank."

"I'll be right there," Aaron promised.

While he waited on his partner, Cole called the
bunkhouse to tell the cook to send one of the ranch

hands to the north pasture to get the gelding. When he hung up, he briefly thought about calling Paige to let her know about the situation but decided against it. Aside from the fact that he hadn't had the opportunity to talk to Aaron about overseeing the crew making the repairs to the ranch, he hated the idea of her seeing him like this. Nothing made a man feel lower than having a woman witness him at his weakest.

"Did Aaron say what happened to Cole?" Paige asked as she and Stella hurried through the emergency room entrance at Royal Memorial Hospital.

Stella shook her head. "When Aaron called all he told me was to find you, let you know that he was taking Cole to the hospital because he had gotten hurt and to make sure you met them here."

Paige briefly wondered why Cole hadn't called her, but then she realized that after the events of the night before, she would most likely be the last person he'd call. She was not only guilty of initiating their love-making, but she also had been so embarrassed by her actions that she hadn't been able to face him this morning.

It was true that she'd had a breakfast meeting of the planning committee for the Family Crisis Center's annual spring fund-raiser, but wanting to put off having to see the condemnation in Cole's dark green eyes, she'd left the house an hour and a half before it started. She knew she'd taken the coward's way out, and it wasn't something she was the least bit proud of. But she had no idea what she would say to him in the way of an explanation for her actions when she didn't fully understand them herself.

Her inner turmoil had seemed to set the tone for the rest of her morning. During the meeting she had learned she would need to present a program outlining the charity's objectives and accomplishments for the newer volunteers. Public speaking was something she hated doing and was much more comfortable working in the background while others took charge. But with so many in need of assistance after the tornado, all the volunteers were having to take charge of this or that in order to meet the needs of the people they were trying to help.

Now Cole had been injured and it wasn't quite noon. She was almost afraid of what the afternoon would bring.

"Could you please tell me if Cole Richardson has arrived yet?" Paige asked when she and Stella approached the reception desk.

"Are you family?" the receptionist asked politely.

Technically she supposed they were family, but Paige wasn't sure they would allow a sister-in-law in the treatment room or tell her anything about his condition. "I'm Mrs. Richardson."

The woman smiled. "Your husband was brought in about fifteen minutes ago by his business partner. Mr. Nichols is with him now, but you can go on back. He's in examination room twenty-four." She shook her head apologetically at Stella. "I'm afraid only two can be in the room with him at a time."

"No problem," Stella assured the woman. When

Paige started toward the entrance leading to the treatment rooms, Stella stopped her. "Please tell Aaron that I'll be in the waiting room."

"I will." Paige hugged her friend as she whispered, "And thank you for not correcting the receptionist's assumption."

"You and Cole are all the family either of you have left," Stella stated quietly. "Under similar circumstances, I would have done the same thing." She smiled. "Now, go back there to see what's going on and send my handsome husband out here to keep me company."

Smiling, Paige nodded and walked back to the room where Cole was being treated. "What happened?" she asked when she reached the cubicle where Cole lay on a hospital bed. His eyes were closed and she couldn't tell where he was injured.

Standing beside the bed, Aaron turned to smile at her. "He decided to try being a cowboy again and ride a horse. But he found out he's just a little rusty."

She frowned. "He went horseback riding?"

Aaron shrugged. "When he called he said he'd been riding along the creek and the bank collapsed. The horse went one way and Cole went the other."

"Does he have a concussion?" she asked, concerned that Cole hadn't opened his eyes.

"As hard-headed and stubborn as he can be sometimes, he might have been better off if he had landed on his head," Aaron answered, chuckling. "But he apparently tried a standing dismount and couldn't quite stick the landing. He screwed up his knee and we're waiting for Lucas Wakefield to examine him and let us know how bad it is."

"But this wouldn't be serious enough for Luc to be called in, would it?" she asked. Dr. Wakefield was head of the trauma department and the region's top trauma surgeon.

Aaron shook his head. "Aaron was with me when I got Cole's call, and you know how we all are. TCC members take care of our own. Once Luc found out Cole was injured, he wanted to see him first."

"Hey, sweetheart," Cole said, opening his eyes to give her a big grin. "Did you come to give me a good-night kiss?"

Shocked, Paige's cheeks burned with embarrassment. "It's not quite noon yet, Cole." When she looked at Aaron, she asked, "Are you sure he didn't land on his head?"

Winking at her, Aaron laughed out loud. "They gave him something for pain and I think he's starting to feel the effects," he explained. When Cole reached for her hand, Aaron nodded toward the door. "You can take over from here with Don Juan. I'll be out in the waiting room if you need me."

"Stella's out there waiting for you," Paige said as Cole took her hand in his to pull her closer. She waited until Aaron had left the room before she tried to extricate her hand from Cole's. She would have tried sooner, but she was afraid of what Cole would say. "Why don't you try to get some rest, Cole?"

"Why don't you climb into bed with me and we'll

rest together?" he asked, giving her another goofy grin as he tried to pull her closer.

"The nurses and doctor won't let me," she said, thankful that the bed rail was between them. Even with him under the influence of a painkiller, she was no match for his strength. "Besides, you don't mean that."

"Yes, I do." He looked for all the world as if he did indeed mean it.

"We'll discuss this later," she said when Lucas Wakefield walked into the room.

Confident that Cole was in good hands, Paige started to leave the room so Luc could examine Cole's leg. "I'll be in the waiting room with Stella and Aaron."

"Stay here," Cole insisted.

She shook her head. "I can't. Luc needs to examine your leg."

"You don't have to leave," Luc said, smiling as he lifted the sheet to look at Cole's swollen right knee. With practiced yet gentle hands, he tried to bend Cole's leg as Paige looked on. When it appeared that it was locked in place, Luc shook his head. "I'm almost positive you've torn the meniscus. I'm going to order a MRI and call in an orthopedic colleague of mine for a consultation. Depending on what the MRI shows and what the orthopedist says, we may be doing surgery."

"Okaaay," Cole said, sounding drowsy. Apparently the full effect of the drug was going to put him to sleep.

"Surely you won't do the surgery today, will you?" Paige asked, alarmed.

"Normally, we wait until we see if the problem resolves itself on its own. That usually takes two or three weeks," Luc explained to her after it was apparent Cole had fallen asleep. "But the way his knee is locked, I'm afraid a piece of the meniscus may have been torn off and possibly lodged in the joint. That won't get better without surgery." He walked to the door. "I'll go put the order in with Imaging and talk to you again after we get the results of the MRI."

Within fifteen minutes a technician from the imaging department arrived to wheel Cole down the hall for the MRI, leaving Paige to sit down in a chair in the corner and wait for his return. It was the first chance she had to think about his reaction when he'd opened his eyes to find her standing next to the bed.

He'd seemed genuinely glad to see her, and that surprised her. Of course, he was under the influence of strong pain medication, but she always thought that drugs tended to remove filters and revealed what a person really felt. Could it be that he wasn't as upset about last night as she thought he would be? If that was the case, why had he been so pensive after they made love? Was he as confused about what happened as she was? And why hadn't he called her instead of Aaron?

"Paige, I've admitted Cole and he's being taken up to the surgical floor," Luc said, walking back into the small examination room almost an hour later.

Lost in thought, she hadn't realized so much time had passed. "I take it that your diagnosis was confirmed?" she asked, standing up.

"It's not quite as bad as it could have been," Luc said as they walked out into the hall. "I used a little of my pull and had the radiologist give it a preliminary look.

He said the meniscus is torn and ragged and looks like it needs to be trimmed so that it doesn't get caught in the joint."

"When will you be doing surgery?" she asked.

"Tomorrow." Luc smiled. "I'll be observing, and Dr. Campbell will be the attending surgeon. He's the orthopedic specialist I called in. I'll only be observing because of my friendship with Cole."

"I suppose it's because Cole is a TCC member and so are you that you're going to be in the operating room with him?" she guessed.

Luc nodded. "Members of the TCC tend to look out for each other."

"Is that also why the surgery was scheduled so quickly?" There was a bond between TCC members unlike anything she had ever seen.

"Partly," Luc said. "If it was anyone else, we'd probably send him home and schedule the surgery within a week or two. But I know Cole. Given the opportunity, he'll put it off because he's too busy with work to be bothered. Unfortunately, that could cause more damage."

"In other words, you aren't going to give him a choice," she said, knowing that what Luc said was right on the mark. Cole was so dedicated to R&N Builders he bordered on being a workaholic.

"Well, let's just say instead of not giving him a choice, we're sending him a strong message that it's something he doesn't want to delay," Luc answered, laughing. "Besides, it will be arthroscopic surgery and relatively simple. You'll be able to take him home tomorrow afternoon. But he'll have to stay off that leg and keep it elevated for a few days to keep the swelling down."

Paige wondered how Cole would take the news that she was going to take care of his recovery. Because she was the closest thing to family that he had, she was the obvious choice. "Does Cole know about all of this?"

"I told him right after we took a look at the MRI." Luc laughed. "I thought I'd better tell him and get him to sign the consent forms while he was between doses of pain medication and relatively lucid."

Paige smiled. "That was probably a good idea. He's not quite himself once he takes that."

"Most people aren't," Luc said. "Looks like duty calls," he said as a nurse approached with a metal chart in her hand. "I'll see you first thing in the morning, Paige."

As she walked down the hall toward the waiting room to tell Aaron and Stella about the surgery, she couldn't help but think about the upcoming week or so. The first few days might not be too bad. Cole would be on painkillers to keep him comfortable. And if his behavior today was any indication, they wouldn't be discussing their indiscretion; she would be trying to avoid another one.

But there wasn't a doubt in her mind that there would be a day of reckoning when he had recovered enough to stop taking the medication. She just hoped things weren't extremely uncomfortable for either of them when that day came.

* * *

The following morning, Paige sat in a corner by herself in the surgical waiting area while Cole was in surgery. She had spent a restless night thinking about what would happen when she took him back to the ranch. There was no way she was going to try to get him upstairs to his bedroom. There were too many steps and she could only imagine how hazardous it might prove to be with him using a set of crutches.

"Have they taken Cole back to the OR?" Lark Taylor asked when she walked into the waiting room.

Looking up at the pretty registered nurse, Paige nodded. "They took him into surgery about ten minutes ago." She smiled. "I didn't expect to see you today, Lark."

"I'm on break and thought I would come out and check on you," Lark answered. "It won't take too long, and Cole's in the very best hands possible," Lark assured her as she lowered herself onto the chair next to Paige. "Dr. Campbell is the best orthopedic surgeon on this side of the state, and you know Luc Wakefield's reputation. Both of them are top-notch."

"I have no doubt everything will go well." Paige gave Lark a meaningful smile. "I'm just wondering how much of a bear Cole is going to be during his recovery."

The nurse laughed. "Men will be men. I haven't seen one yet who isn't a total grouch when he's sick or injured."

"How are the wedding plans coming?" Paige asked as their laughter faded. Lark was engaged to Keaton

Holt, another member of the TCC, and Paige had never seen the woman happier.

Lark's green eyes sparkled with excitement. "Our families are working together for a change and I think it's actually going to come together by June. Of course, it didn't hurt that Keaton told everyone they better not disappoint me or they'd have him to deal with."

Paige was a bit surprised that things between the two families were so harmonious. The Taylors and Holts had been feuding for some time and it had surprised everyone when Lark and Keaton had fallen in love.

As she stared at Lark, Paige couldn't help but feel envious. The woman was about to marry the man she loved with all her heart, and her excitement was palpable. Looking back on her own wedding day, Paige wished she could say that she had been happy about starting a new life with Craig. But all she could remember feeling was a deep sense of desolation. She had disappointed her parents and had been entering into a marriage with a man she didn't love and who didn't love her. It was supposed to have been the happiest day of her life, but for her it had been one of the saddest.

"You and Cole will be there, won't you?" Lark asked, looking hopeful.

"I can't speak for Cole, but I wouldn't miss your wedding for anything, Lark," Paige said, forcing a smile. "Do you have a gift registry at any of the shops in town?"

"Keaton and I really don't need anything, so I didn't bother," Lark said, shaking her head. "We've decided to request that in lieu of a wedding gift, we'd like for everyone to make a donation to the Royal Tornado Relief Fund or the Family Crisis Center."

"That's such a wonderful idea," Paige said sincerely. "There are still so many in need. I'm sure that both charities will be very appreciative. And I know firsthand they can put the extra money to good use."

"That's what we thought." Lark checked her watch. "My break is almost over. I need to get back to the ICU," she said, rising to her feet. "Good luck taking care of Cole while he recovers from his surgery. And if you need any help or have questions about it, please let me know."

"I will," Paige said, standing to give her friend a hug.

As she watched Lark, who was so thrilled about her upcoming wedding and future, walk out of the waiting room, she felt guilty. Even though she and Craig hadn't been in love, he had been a good husband and the only thing he had ever asked of her was to watch over his father while he was out of town on business. He couldn't help that her heart had been elsewhere on their wedding day or that she had felt as if she were marrying the wrong brother.

Her heart stalled and she gave herself a mental shake. It was water under the bridge now, and there was no sense in dwelling on the mistakes of the past.

As she sat back down to wait for Luc to come out and tell her how Cole's surgery had gone, she thought about the mistake she had made the other night with Cole. It wasn't so much that she felt their lovemaking was wrong. Nothing in her life had felt more right than what she had shared with Cole. It was the circumstances leading up to it that bothered her the most—the fact that she had practically thrown herself at him. What was there about the man that made her act so out of character?

"Cole came through the surgery just fine," Luc said, interrupting her thoughts. Still dressed in his blue surgical scrubs, he walked over to her and sat down. "He's just coming out of recovery and as soon as he gets dressed, you can take him home."

"Is there anything special that I need to do?" She shook her head. "Let me rephrase that. Is there anything I need to try to prevent Cole from doing?"

Nodding, Luc chuckled. "It probably won't be easy, but if you can, keep him off his feet for the next few days. Cole will be on crutches and that should help, but he needs to keep his leg elevated to prevent swelling. Dr. Campbell has a list of instructions that he sends home with his patients, along with a prescription for pain medication. He's also made arrangements for in-home physical therapy to start on Monday. You can call when you get home and set up a time." Luc stood up to leave. "Cole will have a follow-up appointment at the end of next week, but if you need anything or have a concern before then, don't hesitate to get in touch with me."

"Does that include calling you to come by and give him a lecture when he fails to listen to me?" she joked.

"If he gets too ornery, I'll come out to the ranch and help you hog-tie him," Luc said, laughing.

Listening to Luc, Paige decided there would be plenty of time later to analyze what there was about Cole that caused her to react the way she did. Right now, she needed to take him back to the ranch and see just how difficult it was going to be getting him to follow doctor's orders.

Five

"Dammit," Cole muttered as he tried to get up the back porch steps. He couldn't use his right leg and he was convinced his crutches were a bigger hindrance than they were help.

"Do you need to lean on me?" Paige asked from behind him.

"No, I can make it," he answered through gritted teeth. He was determined to get up the damned steps on his own or die trying. He wasn't about to accept her help.

By the time he made it onto the porch, sweat beaded his forehead, and he'd silently run through every cuss word he had ever heard. He couldn't think of anything more humiliating than for Paige to see his helplessness. No man wanted a woman to see how inadequate and weak he was—struggling to do even the basics. It didn't just bruise his ego; it took a seriously large chunk out of it.

While he stood there catching his breath and feeling lower than the stuff he scraped off his boots after a trip through the barnyard, she opened the back door for him to enter the kitchen. Following her through the house on the crutches was torturous, and by the time he got to the family room, Cole knew that physically he'd gone about as far as he could go without sitting down to rest.

"I anticipated climbing stairs being a problem for you," she said as he made his way across the room. "That's why we're not going to attempt getting you up to your room."

He shook his head. "I'll make it. I just need to rest a little."

"No, you won't." She pointed to the couch. "I've already pulled this out into a bed and I've added a four-inch-thick memory foam mattress topper to make it more comfortable for you."

"You didn't need to go to all this trouble," he said, secretly relieved that she wouldn't be watching him struggle to get up the stairs. He might have protested, but as he eyed the bed, he had to admit he was more than ready to lie down after the ordeal of getting from the car into the house.

"Don't be silly," she said, taking his crutches and setting them aside when he lowered himself to the edge of the sofa sleeper. "It's no trouble at all."

Even though he was having a hard time accepting

his limitations, he was thankful for Paige's foresight. She had not only made him a bed downstairs, she'd sent Aaron to the sporting goods store to pick up the pair of gym shorts he was now wearing. There was no way he could have gotten up all those stairs on crutches without falling and breaking his neck, nor could he have put on a pair of jeans. The bandage on his knee alone would have prevented that. But there was an added bonus in wearing the shorts. Because he was going to be in the family room and couldn't go to bed in the buff as he normally did, he could wear them to sleep in, as well.

"Thanks for everything," he said, being careful when he stretched out not to cause himself any more pain than he was already in. His knee was killing him, and he was more than ready for some of the pain pills Dr. Campbell had prescribed for him.

"You need some of your medication, don't you?" she asked as she arranged pillows under his leg to elevate it.

Nodding, he closed his eyes against the throbbing in his knee. "If you don't mind, I really would appreciate it."

As she left the room, Cole wondered how things could get more complicated. He was not only laid up for the next week or so, he was being cared for by his brother's wife—the woman he had taken advantage of when she had turned to him for comfort. And even though she had asked him to make love to her, he'd been well aware of the fact that she had been frightened and vulnerable. He should have been stronger—should have been able to keep his head and resist. He fully intended to talk to her and offer a heartfelt apol-

ogy for his lapse in judgment when the pain in his knee
calmed down to a manageable level. He just hoped like
hell she accepted it.

When she returned from the kitchen with a glass
of water and a couple of the pills, Cole didn't waste
any time downing them as quickly as he could. But he
hated having to rely on medication to escape the pain. It
made him sleepy and he couldn't remember a damned
thing from the time they kicked in until they wore off
and he had to take more. But there was an added ben-
efit. At least he didn't have to see the pity in Paige's
pretty gray eyes—or if he did, he didn't remember it.

"Try to get some sleep," she advised as she carefully
pulled the sheet up to his waist. She placed a small
handbell on the end table beside the sofa. "If you need
anything, all you have to do is ring this bell."

As he watched her leave the room, he breathed a
sigh of relief. At least she hadn't asked why he'd gone
out riding yesterday or mentioned anything about wanting to discuss the other night. It was something they
needed and would do, but not until he felt as though
he could talk without clenching his teeth against the
throbbing in his knee.

Closing his eyes again, Cole felt as if he were float-
ing and knew the medication was starting to kick in.
As he drifted off to sleep, he smiled. Even though he
was sure he came up lacking in her eyes, there wasn't
a thing about Paige that he didn't find absolutely
amazing. With her long, dark auburn hair framing
her angel face and her gray eyes filled with concern

for him, he didn't think he'd ever seen a woman as beautiful or enticing as his Paige.

Thirty minutes after she'd given Cole the medication, Paige went back into the family room to check on him. She knew that he was embarrassed and not at all happy that she was having to take care of him. But she enjoyed feeling needed again. Her own mother had always told her she was a natural-born nurturer and would be a wonderful mother someday. Because it appeared that was never going to happen, she had to be content nurturing others she cared for.

Craig had never made her feel that he really needed her, and if she hadn't had Mr. Richardson to focus her attention on while Craig was away, she couldn't imagine how boring her life would have been. But Cole and Craig's father had always made her feel as if she made a difference in the quality of his life, and toward the end, she was the one he'd asked to oversee his diet, medications and doctor's appointments. He'd even told her it was nice to have a woman fuss over him again—something he hadn't had since his wife had died when the twins were little.

As Paige walked over to the bed to stare down at Cole, she smiled. The boy she thought to be so good-looking when they were in high school was nothing compared to the devastatingly handsome man he had become.

Why couldn't he have been the Richardson twin to ask her out all those years ago? He had promised her that he would wait the two years for her to graduate from school. Why hadn't he come back home that summer and kept his promise? And why hadn't she waited for him?

Paige sighed over what might have been. If there had been even the slightest possibility of a second chance for them, she had ruined it. From the moment he came back to Royal over six months ago, Cole had avoided being with her, and it had been clear that he hadn't wanted to stay at the Double R. But she had pressured him into agreeing simply because she had been so lonely. Then when he'd tried to be a gentleman and help her through the fear she'd had since the tornado, she had pressed for more by asking him to make love to her.

Lost in thought, she was startled when Cole reached up to grab hold of her hand. "Hi, sweetheart. Where have you been?"

"In the kitchen," she answered, knowing that he had no idea where he was, let alone where she had been.

"Why don't you lie down with me and I'll hold you while it storms," he said, giving her the same grin he had when she'd first seen him in the hospital.

Her breath caught at the reference to their night together. But she immediately dismissed it. It was the medication talking, not Cole.

"It isn't even raining," she said, forcing a smile.

"We can pretend it is," he coaxed, pulling her down to sit on the edge of the bed beside him. He reached up to trace her lips with his forefinger. "That way we can make love again."

"Why don't you try to get some more sleep," she

countered, her pulse racing like a runaway train. To get her mind off his ramblings, she checked to make sure his leg was still elevated.

When he closed his eyes and she thought he had drifted back to sleep, she started to get up. But his eyes flew open, and he tightened his grip on her hand. "I sleep better and I'm a lot happier when you're with me." His grin widened. "We could make love again."

"That wouldn't be a good idea." Thinking fast, she added, "I don't want to run the risk of hurting your knee."

She knew his euphoria was drug-induced and that he didn't have a clue what he was saying. But that didn't keep her from wishing that he did.

"I, um, have a few things I need to do," she said, trying hard to come up with a convincing excuse. "Would it help if I sit here until you go back to sleep?"

He looked disappointed but finally nodded. "I just don't want to lose you again," he said sleepily.

He didn't want to lose her again? What did he mean by that?

She tried not to put too much stock in what Cole said. He wasn't himself on the medication and nothing he said was based in reality. Unfortunately, her heart wanted to argue the point.

Paige waited until she was absolutely certain Cole was asleep before she extricated her hand from his, stood up and left the family room. She had to call Royal Memorial Hospital to set up an appointment for the following week with an in-home therapist to start Cole's physical therapy. Then she needed to start the chicken soup she'd planned for their dinner. And if she could think of something else to do, she'd do that, too. The busier she kept herself, the less time she would have to think about the man softly snoring on her pullout couch.

Two hours later, she checked on the soup simmering on top of the stove and finished filling parfait cups with chocolate pudding when she heard the ringing of the bell she'd left beside the bed. Putting the cups into the refrigerator, she wiped her hands and hurried into the family room.

"You rang, sir?" she asked, smiling.

"Could you hand me the remote control?" he asked, his eyes not quite meeting hers. "I tried, but I can't reach it without putting pressure on my knee."

"Of course," she said, handing it to him. "Is there anything else I can get for you?"

He shook his head. "I won't bother you again."

"You're not bothering me," she said, smiling. "Just relax and watch the news. I'll bring dinner in to you in a few minutes."

Walking back into the kitchen, she shook her head as she placed bowls of soup, toasted cheese sandwiches and glasses of iced tea on a bed tray to carry into the family room. She had been right. Cole hated that he had to rely on her for the simplest of things. And she could understand that his pride was suffering because of it. But it wouldn't be forever, and if their positions were reversed, she was sure he wouldn't mind helping her.

"Let's get you propped up so you can have dinner," she said when she returned to the family room.

"Thanks, but I'm not really hungry," he said, continuing to stare at the television.

"You have to eat something," she said, setting the tray on the coffee table she'd moved out of the way when she'd pulled out the sofa bed before going to the hospital that morning. Reaching for some throw pillows, she smiled. "Do you need me to help you sit up?"

He finally looked up at her. "Really, Paige, I don't want to be a problem."

Frowning, she put her fists on her hips. "Let's get something straight, Cole Richardson. You are not a bother, a burden or a problem. You need someone to take care of you while you recuperate and, whether you like it or not, you're stuck with me. Now, sit up and let me put these pillows behind you so you can eat dinner. And don't tell me you aren't hungry. I happen to know you haven't had anything to eat all day."

He looked surprised by her outburst, but instead of arguing the matter further, he managed to sit up on his own without putting pressure on his knee and leaned forward for her to put the pillows behind his back. "I hope you didn't go to a lot of trouble."

She smiled. "None at all. The instructions Dr. Campbell sent home with you suggested a soft diet this evening because of the anesthesia, so I kept it very simple and easy." She picked up the bed tray and, being careful not to bump his knee, placed it over his thighs. "You have homemade chicken soup, a toasted cheese sandwich and iced tea." She picked up her dinner from the tray, carried it over to the armchair and sat down.

"Be sure to save room for dessert. I made chocolate pudding."

"Thank you," he said, picking up his spoon to taste the soup. After he swallowed, he said, "Normally I don't care much for soup, but this is really good."

She hid a smile as she watched him eat. For someone who claimed he wasn't very hungry, Cole had downed the bowl of soup and devoured the sandwich in record time.

"Would you like some more soup or another sandwich?" she asked, placing her empty bowl with his on the tray to take back to the kitchen.

"I think I'd rather have the pudding," he said, giving her the first smile she'd seen from him today that wasn't under the influence of pain pills.

"I'll be right back with it," she said, returning his smile.

While they ate their pudding, they watched one of the military investigation dramas on TV, and by the time the show was over, she could tell he needed more pain medication. After giving him one of the pills, she sat back down in the armchair to wait until Cole dozed off before she went back into the kitchen to clean up.

"If you have something else you need to do, go ahead," he said, yawning. "I'll be fine."

Rising to her feet, she motioned toward the kitchen. "I'll go ahead and clean up from dinner. If you need me—"

"I'll ring…the bell," he said, closing his eyes. He sounded extremely sleepy, and she knew he was moments away from going to sleep.

Fifteen minutes later, after wiping down the counter and starting the dishwasher, Paige returned to the family room. She gasped when she found Cole trying to get out of the bed. "Where do you think you're going?" she asked, alarmed that he might hurt himself further.

"I was coming to find you," he said, grinning from ear to ear. "I can't sleep without you."

"Why don't you try?" If he was going to attempt to find her whenever she wasn't in the room with him, it was going to be a big problem. She might just have to curl up in the armchair for the night.

He stubbornly shook his head and started to get up again.

"What if I sit beside you and we watch a little more TV together?" she suggested. Maybe if she humored him, he'd relax and drift off for the night. Then once she was sure he was sound asleep, she would get up and move back to the armchair.

That seemed to placate him, so she took off her shoes, went over to the other side of the bed and, propping some throw pillows behind her, stretched out her legs on the mattress. As they watched another crime drama, Paige couldn't help but think about the difference in Cole when he was on the pain medication. Once he took one of the capsules it wasn't long before he was as happy as a lark and willing to go along with just about everything she suggested.

But he wouldn't be zonked out on painkillers forever. Yawning, she briefly wondered how much longer he would need them. Probably not more than another day or so at best. She just hoped his disposition improved when his discomfort eased. The smiling, affable Cole was much easier to deal with than the grouch he could be when the medication wore off.

Maybe then they could discuss what had happened the other night, she could apologize for her role in the matter and they could move on.

When Cole woke up it didn't take long for him to realize he wasn't in bed alone. Paige's head was resting on his shoulder and his arm was around her. He briefly wondered how the hell they had gotten that way. The last thing he remembered was taking another dose of pain medication and lying back to watch an episode of his favorite television show. Paige had been sitting in the armchair just a few feet away.

How did she end up in bed with him and why? He'd bet every dime he had it hadn't been her idea. Did that mean the pain pills had him doing something besides just sleeping? If that was the case, he'd taken the last of the pain pills, no matter how much his knee hurt.

"Paige," he said softly, not wanting to startle her. "It's time to wake up."

He watched her blink a moment before she tilted her head to look up at him. Her eyes widened as she realized where she was.

"Oh, Cole, I'm so sorry," she apologized as she tried to pull away from him. "I must have fallen asleep while we watched TV. Is your knee all right? Is it still elevated? I'll get up and get you some more of your medication."

"Slow down, Paige," he said, tightening his arm

around her to hold her in place. "Yes, my knee is sore but it's not intolerable right now. Yes, it's still elevated. And no, I don't need any more of that damned medication. I have a feeling it's responsible for you being in bed with me." He took a deep breath. "Exactly what did I do or say while I was under its influence?"

"Let me get out of bed and we'll talk," she said, pushing on his chest again.

This time he released her and struggled to sit up without moving his knee. Glancing at the clock on the mantel, he realized it was just before dawn. Had they spent the entire night in bed together?

"What time did you get in bed with me?" he asked.

"I'm going to start a pot of coffee," she said, brushing her long hair back away from her eyes with both hands. "Then we can talk." If she was evading his questions like this, it wasn't a good sign.

"That might not be a bad idea," he said, hoping the caffeine would clear his head and help him remember the events of the night before.

He didn't like being unable to remember what he'd said or done. It made him feel out of control— something he tried never to allow himself to be.

A sudden thought had his heart pounding hard against his ribs. Surely they hadn't made love again. He glanced down at his T-shirt and gym shorts. He was pretty sure they hadn't. For one thing, they were both fully dressed. And for another, she seemed just as surprised to be waking up in his arms as he was to be holding her.

"Would you like for me to make your breakfast?"

Paige asked, walking back into the room with two mugs of coffee. "I know you must be hungry."

He figured her offering to fix breakfast was her way of putting off talking to him. "Not right now. I want answers more than I want something to eat."

She stared at him a moment before she gave a short nod and walked over to sit in the armchair. "What do you want to know?"

"Just exactly how bizarre do I get when I'm on the pain medication?" he asked, taking a sip of his coffee.

"I wouldn't really call it bizarre," she said, shaking her head. "The only thing I can think of that was a little scary was when you tried to get out of bed."

He frowned. "Do you know why I was trying to get up?"

She nodded. "You were trying to find me."

"Was there something I needed?" he prompted. Her abbreviated answers indicated there was something she didn't want to tell him. He was determined to find out what that something was.

She shook her head but didn't quite look him in the eyes. "You just wanted me to be in here with you."

"What else?" He set his cup on the end table and carefully lowered his legs over the side of the bed to sit on the edge. "And don't tell me there isn't something. You're too reluctant to talk to me about it for there not to be."

She took a sudden interest in the contents of the cup in her hand. "Really, that was the only thing you did."

"What did I say?" he asked, knowing when she

jerked her head up to look at him that he'd hit pay dirt. "And why were you in bed with me?"

"You kept asking me to get into bed with you because you said you slept better when I was there." She shrugged one slender shoulder. "You were so insistent that I told you I would sit beside you while we watched television. I must have fallen asleep because the next thing I remember was waking up with my head on your shoulder."

"I've been on that medication for two days," he said slowly. "There has to be more."

She sighed audibly. "You really want to know?"

"I wouldn't have asked if I didn't," he said firmly.

"You might not like some of it," she warned.

"Just tell me, Paige."

"In the ER you asked if I had come to kiss you goodnight," she said, smiling as if she found the incident humorous. "That was the first indication Aaron and I had that this medication might be causing a personality change in you."

"Aaron heard that?"

His friend was never going to let Cole hear the end of that one. Fortunately, he had gathered a few things on Aaron over the years that were just as embarrassing and when mentioned would shut him up in a hurry.

She nodded. "But he walked out of the room just before you tried to get me to climb into the hospital bed with you."

Cole groaned. "Was that it?"

"That was all that happened at the hospital," she

said, nodding. "The majority of what you said was here after I brought you home from the hospital."

So far it wasn't as bad as it could have been. "You might as well tell me everything."

"Every time you take the medication you want me to get into bed with you," she said, her cheeks coloring a pretty pink.

"I'm nothing if not persistent," he muttered, disgusted with himself. "Is that it?"

She hesitated before she continued. "A couple of times when you tried to talk me into getting into bed with you, you wanted us to make love again."

Outstanding, he thought sarcastically. Apparently, under the influence of the drug he was quite chatty.

"I know you didn't mean it," she said hurriedly. She paused for a moment, and then took a deep breath. "And as long as we're talking about making love, I'm really sorry about the other night." She stared down at her hands. "I more or less threw myself at you and I take full responsibility."

He shook his head. "Paige, there's absolutely no reason for you to apologize. I took advantage of the situation."

"No, you didn't." She got up from the chair and reached for his empty coffee cup. "I practically begged you to make love to me, and the next morning I was so embarrassed by my actions, I left the house early to go to my meeting just so I wouldn't have to face you."

Cole knew she was going to try to escape to the kitchen, but he was determined to get everything out in the open. Taking the cups from her hand, he set them on the end table, then pulled her down to sit beside him on the side of the bed. To keep from taking her in his arms, he gripped the edge of the mattress with both hands.

"Paige, don't you get it? If I hadn't wanted to make love to you the other night, there's nothing you could have said or done to change my mind," he stated flatly. "Give me credit for having more control."

"You did try to talk me out of it," she insisted. "You were obviously reluctant and I ignored that."

"Did you hear what I just said?" he asked. "I just told you I wanted to make love to you, Paige. Hell, if the truth is known, I've wanted you since I first laid eyes on you walking down the hall at Royal High School."

"You wanted me?" she asked, looking as if she couldn't quite believe it.

Nodding, he gave up and put his arm around her shoulders. "You're my late brother's wife and the two of you would still be married if that tornado hadn't come through six months ago and taken Craig's life. I've disrespected Craig's memory and your marriage and I'm truly sorry for that. But as contradictory as it sounds, I'll be damned if I regret that it happened."

"I don't, either," she said, surprising him. "I still feel like we wouldn't have made love if I hadn't pressed the matter, but what we shared was absolutely beautiful."

They sat in silence for a few minutes as reality set in. "So where do we go from here?" he finally asked.

"I suppose we could go back to building a nice friendship," Paige answered, sounding a little unsure.

He shook his head. "Sweetheart, I don't think that's possible."

She looked disappointed. "Why not?"

"I know I shouldn't and I've fought it with everything that's in me because you're my late brother's wife, but I want to be a whole lot more to you than just your friend, Paige," he said, lowering his head to capture her soft coral lips with his. "That's why I don't think a friendship between us would even be possible."

Not wanting to start something he couldn't finish, Cole made sure to keep the kiss simple and sweet. It was still unclear how things were going to progress between them or if they even wanted to try for something more. And there was no way he needed to add a boatload of frustration to the discomfort from his throbbing knee.

When he raised his head, he smiled. "You mentioned something about making breakfast?"

She looked as unsure about his declaration as he felt when she nodded. "What would you like to have?"

"It doesn't matter to me." He grinned. "I'm about as hungry as a bear waking up from hibernation. Even though it was really good, soup doesn't stick with you for very long."

Her smile was one of the prettiest sights he'd ever seen. "I'll go see what I can whip up."

As he watched her leave the room, Cole had no idea where things were going with them or how it would all turn out. Even though Craig would have had no problem making a move on Paige if the situation had been reversed and she had been his widow, Cole still couldn't help but have some lingering guilt about his feelings for her. But he also knew that if he didn't stick around and find out where their attraction led them, he would end up regretting it for the rest of his life.

Six

"Cole, I don't think this is what the doctors had in mind when he said to take it easy and keep your leg elevated," Paige observed as they walked toward the men working on her barn. His progress was slow, but Cole did seem to be getting the hang of using the crutches.

"I promise if my knee starts to hurt more than it does right now, I'll have the guys help me back inside," he said, giving her a smile that caused her pulse to race.

As soon as his men had called to tell him they were all fully recovered from the food poisoning and ready to go back to work, he decided one of them could set up a couple of lawn chairs under the live oak tree closest to the barn so that Cole could oversee their work. After trying to talk him out of it with no success, she finally gave in and carried the pillow for him to put under his leg when he propped it up on the other chair.

"What if it starts raining?" she asked as he lowered himself into the lawn chair and laid his crutches on the ground beside him. "You're not supposed to get the bandage wet."

"Do you worry this much over everything?" he asked, laughing.

"Your father used to call it fussing." She smiled at the fond memory as she placed the pillow she had under her arm on the chair facing Cole. "He used to tell me I fussed over everything."

"Well, I'm sure he loved having you around 'fussing' over him," Cole commented. "Dad didn't get much of that after Mom died."

"That's what he'd told me." Helping Cole get his leg positioned comfortably in the chair, she added, "But I didn't mind at all. We became quite close over the years, and I really miss him."

When she turned to go back to the house, Cole caught her hand in his to stop her. "Thank you for taking care of my dad when his health started to fail," he said, his expression turning serious. "I'm glad he had you here with him."

"No need to thank me. I enjoyed spending the time with him," she said, smiling. As an afterthought, she warned, "Oh, I almost forgot to remind you. Don't be so stubborn about working that you overdo things. If you do, you might need to start taking the medication again."

"There you go fussing again," Cole teased. His

grin caused a tiny shiver to slide up her spine. "Don't worry. I'm done with those pills. I don't care how much it hurts—I want to remember everything I say or do from now on."

Impulsively, she touched his cheek. "Just please take it easy. I'd hate to have to get stern with you again like I did yesterday afternoon when you kept apologizing for being a problem."

He laughed. "Do you have any idea how cute you are when you're laying down the law?"

"I prefer to think of it as being assertive," she said, enjoying their easy banter.

"Boss, here's the blueprints for the barn," one of Cole's men said, walking over with several rolls of paper. He nodded at Paige. "Mornin', ma'am."

After returning the man's greeting, Paige smiled at Cole. "I'll let you get to work and I'll start thinking about what I'm going to make for you and your crew for lunch."

As she walked back to the house, she thought about her talk with Cole earlier that morning and how different he was than before he'd had his accident. He seemed more relaxed around her now, as if confessing that he felt guilty—but that he had no regrets about their making love—had been liberating for him. He had even started showing her small gestures of affection—touching her hand when he talked to her and freely calling her sweetheart. She found she enjoyed the attention and she couldn't help but compare how differently the twin brothers treated her.

Craig had never gone out of his way to be overly affectionate. She frowned at the memory. In fact, it had seemed as if he didn't see the need in showing her any kind of affection unless they were getting ready to have sex. And she couldn't remember Craig ever using an endearment instead of her name.

Her breath caught when she realized how different making love with Cole had been, as well. He'd been gentle and caring, and she'd actually felt as if he cherished her, whereas Craig had been only mildly interested in whether or not she found their times together satisfying.

Of course, she couldn't blame him entirely for the state of their marriage. She had stayed in the loveless union for two very good reasons. First of all, she hadn't wanted to add to her parents' disappointment in her by divorcing Craig. And second, she had made a lifetime commitment to stay with Craig when she'd recited their wedding vows. She had been taught all of her life that it was a promise that wasn't made lightly, nor should it be broken easily.

But Craig was gone and with his death, so was her commitment to honoring their wedding vows. Cole had mentioned wanting to be more to her than just a friend. Was he talking about a future that included her in his life? Or did he mean only while he was staying on the ranch with her?

If that was the case—if he only wanted a casual relationship that would end when he went back to Dallas—she was certain that wouldn't be enough for her. Maybe it was her conservative upbringing or the fact that she had only been with one other man in her life.

But it didn't matter. She never had been, nor would she ever be, the "no-strings-attached" type.

Deciding that only time would tell, she went about her morning as usual. After giving her hired hands a list of chores that needed to be done, she returned to the house to start making lunch for Cole and his men. As she put the finishing touches on a tray of ham-and-cheese sandwiches, she was startled to see one of Cole's men helping him through the back door. Glancing at the clock, she frowned. He had only been outside for a few hours.

"Is your knee hurting?" she asked as she accepted the pillow his worker handed her.

Cole shrugged. "Nothing I can't handle."

The sudden sound of thunder rumbling overhead provided a clue as to why he was returning to the house so soon. "It sounds like the rain is coming early today," she commented.

Cole nodded. "I figured as slow as I am on these damned crutches I'd better get inside before the down-pour started." After he thanked his worker for carrying the chairs to the porch and opening the door for him, Cole grinned. "I didn't want to run the risk of getting another lecture."

Before the man helping Cole went back outside, Paige stopped him. "I already have sandwiches made. Why don't you take them with you for the crew's lunch." She quickly wrapped the sandwiches, put them into a bag and handed it to him. "I hope you like ham and cheese."

"Thank you, ma'am," the man said politely. He

grinned. "We'll eat just about anything but egg salad out of a vending machine."

"Very wise choice," she said, grinning back at the man.

After the worker left the house, she caught Cole staring at her. "Did I do something wrong?" she asked, confused.

He shook his head. "You like taking care of people, don't you?"

"Everyone needs to feel a sense of purpose," she said, smiling. "Mine is caring for those around me. Besides, I like doing it."

"You mean you like 'fussing' over them," he corrected, grinning.

"Whatever." She stopped laughing when she noticed him wincing. "Are you sure your knee is all right?"

"It's sore, but it's a lot better than it was yesterday," he said, slowly lowering himself to one of the chairs at the table.

She moved another chair in front of him, placed the pillow just so and pointed to his leg. "Elevate."

"Now you're being bossy," he said, laughing.

"No, that was me being assertive." She grinned. "There's a difference."

"What do you have planned for this afternoon?" he asked, lifting his leg onto the pillow as she'd instructed.

"I have to work on this month's program for one of my charity meetings." She smiled as she went to the cabinet for plates to set the table. "I'll bet you're going to take a nap."

When he shook his head, his warm smile made her

feel as if he'd caressed her. "I might do that a little later, but I thought I'd start going through some of those boxes we took out of the closet in your studio."

"It's not a studio yet," she said, laughing.

"It will be as soon as we can get into Royal to pick out new floor tile, paint for the walls and cabinets for storage." He looked thoughtful. "If we can get that done one day next week, then the guys can work outside when it isn't raining and inside when it is."

"How does next Thursday afternoon sound?" she asked, setting the table for lunch. "We can go to the lumberyard after your doctor's appointment."

"That will work." He picked up the glass of iced tea she set in front of him. "When is your next meeting at the TCC clubhouse?"

Paige paused for a moment. "Week after next. That's where the meeting of the Family Crisis Center volunteers is always held. Why?"

"I thought I'd set up a meeting with Aaron to discuss some plans we're considering for R&N Builders." Cole smiled. "We've been talking about opening a branch office here in Royal."

"That would be great." Grinning, Paige carried a platter of sandwiches to the table and sat down. "Now that Aaron is married to the mayor and they're expecting a baby, it would probably be a good idea for them to live in the same town."

Cole laughed. "Yeah, he mentioned that when he took me to the hospital the other day."

As they ate, it suddenly occurred to Paige that she still had no idea why Cole had been out riding the day of the accident. "Cole, you never did tell me why you took one of the horses out for a ride the day you got hurt."

"When I was a kid, I used to go riding whenever I needed to think things through," he answered as he covered her hand with his where it rested on top of the table. "I was trying to decide what I needed to do to make things right between us after making love to you."

She glanced at his knee. "Well, it probably wasn't exactly the way you thought it would work out, but the horse did play a role in our dealing with what happened."

He laughed. "Yeah, I guess you're right. If he hadn't stumbled, I wouldn't have a bum knee and we wouldn't have had our talk this morning about the things I said while I was on painkillers."

Loving the easier atmosphere between them, she grinned. "Do me a favor. The next time you need to think, why don't you try doing it from the porch swing? I don't think it would be nearly as hard on you."

He surprised her when he shook his head. "That wouldn't work."

"Why not?" she asked, her pulse racing when he began to trace slow circles on the back of her hand with the pad of his thumb.

"Because if I played it safe and never got hurt, you wouldn't have anything to fuss over." His deep voice sent heat coursing through her veins.

"I do love to fuss," she admitted, feeling a little breathless. *Especially whenever the one I'm fussing over is you.*

After lunch, Cole sat in the den with his leg resting on an ottoman in the wide space under his father's big walnut desk. Going through a few of the boxes, he found several things of his father's that he wanted to keep and more that could be donated to one of the thrift shops in town.

Staring at the pocket knife his father had always carried, Cole couldn't help but smile as he turned it over in his hand. He couldn't remember a time that his dad hadn't had it with him. The handle had been made from a deer antler, and then carved with a scene of a stag regally standing in the middle of a forest. Cole remembered his dad telling him that his and Craig's grandfather had carried that knife from the time he was twelve years old, and Cole had no trouble believing it. The intricate carving had been worn down over the years but it was still a work of art and something that Cole was more than happy to keep. He placed it alongside his dad's pocket watch and chain and the silver dollar with a bullet hole in the middle that had belonged to his great-great grandfather.

With all of the boxes containing his father's things emptied, Cole reached for the carton of his sports trophies. Along with the high school memorabilia, he found a couple of belt buckles he'd earned from junior rodeo and a baseball signed by a couple of Rangers ball players. But he was mystified at finding a computer flash drive at the bottom of the box. He knew for certain that it wasn't his. He hadn't left anything like that behind when he went off to college. That could only mean that at some point in the past several years Craig had thrown it into the box. He didn't even consider the notion that it had belonged to his father. His dad had hated technology and swore that computers would lead to the ruination of the world.

The drive probably had pictures on it or maybe music. Craig used to like collecting both.

Picking up the device, Cole put it into the USB port of the laptop Paige had said belonged to Craig and opened the directory. Most of the files were labeled by month and it appeared that Craig had been keeping a digital journal. But as Cole scanned the list, one file stood out and caused a sickening dread deep in the pit of his stomach.

Double-clicking on his own name, Cole opened the file to find several documents. When he clicked on the top one in the list, he realized it was one of many emails Craig had sent to him in the past year or so.

A deep sense of guilt settled over Cole as he stared at the heading. When his brother had sent the messages, Cole had deleted every one of them unread. At the time, he hadn't been interested in a thing Craig had to say to him. But now?

Cole stared at the computer screen for several long minutes as he tried to decide what he wanted to do. If he opened the email and discovered that Craig had been trying to reach out and make things right between them, he would never forgive himself for not meeting his brother halfway. But the only way he would know for sure would be to read them.

Before he had a chance to talk himself out of it, Cole quickly read the first message, then sat back in the desk chair to stare off into space. What had he ever done to Craig to inspire such hatred? Why had his twin been determined to taunt and harass him with events of the past, even as adults?

In the email, Craig had been reminding him about the fight they'd had over Paige just before she'd graduated from high school. Cole had been home from college on spring break and somehow Craig had discovered that Cole intended to ask her out after graduation. His twin had apparently decided that he was going to spoil that for Cole and vowed that by midsummer Paige would be dating him and by Christmas he would be sleeping with her.

Cole had done everything he could think of to protect Paige from Craig's sick sibling rivalry, but nothing he had tried had made a difference—not even the broken nose Cole had given Craig with a solid right hook. When it became clear that his brother was still intent on executing his plan to use Paige, Cole had tried feigning indifference in the hope that Craig would think he had lost interest in her and give up. Cole had even gone as far as taking a couple of classes during the summer semester to stay away from Royal and prove he was no longer interested in Paige. But Craig had seen through the ploy and finally convinced her to go out with him for the first time that fall.

Cole had thought about telling Paige what Craig

was up to and the sick game he was playing, but Cole hadn't been certain she would believe him. It was so damned bizarre, even he had a hard time believing the extent of the jealousy that had driven Craig.

Looking back, his brother had always been that way toward him—even when they were small children. If Cole had something, it didn't matter what it was, Craig wanted it. If Cole did or said anything that garnered any kind of praise—either from their father or in school—Craig did his best to take credit for it or diminish Cole's accomplishment in some way.

Over the years, Cole had gotten used to Craig's need to be the center of attention and always be the one who came out on top of every situation. For the most part, he had ignored the rivalry and one-upmanship his twin seemed to thrive on. But when Craig went after Paige as a way to taunt and torment Cole, his brother had crossed the line. That's why Cole had cut Craig out of his life. And with the exception of having to see him at their father's funeral, Cole hadn't spoken to his twin in almost twelve years.

But why would Craig have started emailing him a couple of years ago just to dredge up events that had taken place all those years ago? Surely Craig had realized that Cole had moved on with his life.

The dread he had felt when he first saw his name on the file intensified. Craig never did anything without a reason and if it involved Cole, it was most likely a disturbing one.

As he stared at the list of documents, the last thing he wanted to do was read more of Craig's boasting about how he had won Paige and what a loser Cole was. But if there was the slightest possibility that his brother had shown even a tiny bit of remorse for using her the way he had, Cole wanted to know about it. He wanted to find some indication that somewhere beneath all of the spite and cruelty there was a kernel of good in his brother.

Praying there was something in one of the documents that redeemed Craig, even in the smallest of ways, Cole forced himself to read the rest of the messages. When he finished the last one—dated the day before Craig had been killed—Cole's gut burned with white-hot fury. The extent of Craig's depravity was sickening.

The only reason Craig had emailed Cole the past couple of years was to gloat and tell him that he had never loved Paige and had been unfaithful practically from the day they had gotten married. He had explained that when their father had forced him to marry her, Craig had insisted they move to the Double R Ranch on the pretense of watching over their father. Then, while Craig went out of town to find his pleasure with more exciting women, Paige had been left at home with their dad. He had even mentioned purposely avoiding sex during her most fertile times of the month because a baby would have only tied him to her even tighter than their farce of a marriage already had. Craig had closed the last email by telling Cole that he was planning on leaving her for another woman and that Cole could have her now that Craig was done with her.

Sitting back in the chair, Cole shook his head. How could his brother have been so callous? How could he have treated a wonderful, caring woman like Paige with such disregard?

If he hadn't known how Craig operated, he might have questioned why his brother had continued to send the messages when it was clear he wasn't going to get a reaction from Cole or why he had kept a record of them.

But Craig had always been that way. It was as if he liked keeping something—a trophy of sorts—to remind him of his sick escapades. And he had probably figured that when he and Paige were divorced he would send the box to Cole—increasing the chance that Cole would find the memory device and eventually read the messages. Craig had also known Cole well enough to be reasonably sure that he wouldn't tell Paige because he wouldn't want to hurt her.

Cole wasn't certain how long he sat there trying to come to terms with what he had learned. It didn't matter. Nothing would ever change the facts of what Craig had done, nor the impact it would have on Paige if she ever discovered it.

That's why Cole was going to do his best to see that she never found out what a snake she had been married to. He never wanted Paige to know that all of those out-of-town business trips Craig had taken over the years were nothing more than clandestine meetings with other women. Cole couldn't stand the thought of her going through the kind of emotional pain that revelation would bring about and once again becoming the victim of his brother's arrogance.

"Cole, are you all right?" Paige asked from the doorway.

"Uh, sure." He quickly closed out the file on the laptop, pulled the memory device from the USB port and shoved it into the pocket of his gym shorts. "Why?"

"You looked like you're a million miles away," she said, smiling as she started across the room toward him.

"I was just taking a trip down memory lane," he said, motioning toward the boxes of his father's things.

When she stopped beside him, he didn't hesitate to put his arms around her waist to pull her close. His brother might have been a damned fool, but Cole wasn't. He knew exactly what a wonderful treasure she was.

"Did you get the program for your charity group finished?" he asked.

"Y-yes," she said, sounding a little breathless. "And I had enough time to make dinner afterward."

"I didn't realize it was that late," he said, checking his watch.

Her pretty smile sent his blood pressure up a good twenty points. "How is your knee? Do you think you can sit at the table, or would you rather me serve you dinner in bed again?"

Releasing her, he grinned as he reached for his crutches. "I'm not going to lie to you. My knee hurts, but I think I can make it through dinner before I have to lie down."

"You should have taken a nap this afternoon," she said, preceding him across the foyer and down the hall.

"Actually, I'm glad I didn't," he said, realizing it was true.

As hard as it had been to read those emails, Cole couldn't say he was surprised at finding the evidence of his brother's duplicity. It just proved what Cole had thought for a long time. Craig was a narcissist with little or no conscience—maybe even a sociopath. He had uncaringly used Paige for the sole purpose of making himself feel superior, and Cole couldn't believe he had been beating himself up for the past several days because he felt he had disrespected his brother's memory and marriage.

Cole shook his head. He had no idea where things were going with Paige, but there was one thing he was positive of. From here on out, he was done feeling the slightest bit of guilt or remorse for anything that happened between Paige and him.

After dinner, Cole slowly retreated to the family room, while Paige cleaned up the dishes. He hadn't said as much, but she knew his knee was probably throbbing unmercifully. She had caught him wincing a few times during dinner when he didn't think she was looking, and he didn't try to argue when she suggested he lie down to watch the news.

But when she'd offered to get him some of the pain medication, he had refused. She could understand his reluctance, given the way he reacted to it, but she didn't like to see anyone in pain, especially not Cole.

She nibbled on her lower lip. They joked about her worrying over him, but the truth of the matter was, she wouldn't want it any other way. She loved that Cole allowed her to care for him, loved that he seemed to appreciate her efforts and was more comfortable with her doing things for him.

It was such a contrast to the way Craig had always been when she'd tried to do things for him. The few times he had been ill, Craig had been irritable and hadn't seemed to want her anywhere near him. She had been disappointed at first. But as the years passed by, it had ceased to matter.

Frowning, she chided herself for once again comparing Cole to Craig. They might have been twins, but their personalities were as different as their looks, and it was past time to stop noticing the contrast between the two brothers.

It bothered her a bit that Craig always seemed to come up lacking when she thought about them. He was dead and there was no sense in focusing on his shortcomings in life. Craig couldn't help it that she had fallen for Cole all those years ago before she had even met him.

Deciding to make a conscious effort not to compare the men from now on, Paige turned out the kitchen light and went down the hall to the family room to check on Cole. She found that he had fallen asleep, and she wasn't going to wake him.

But the moment she turned to go over to sit in the armchair, his eyes opened and he reached up to catch her hand in his. "Where are you going, sweetheart?" he asked, grinning.

"Did you take some of the medication?" she asked.

The sound of his rich laughter caused a warm feeling deep inside her. "No, and I don't intend to." He hooked his thumb toward the empty mattress beside him. "Why don't you kick off your shoes and stretch out beside me? We can watch the Rangers game together."

"Who are they playing?" she asked as she slipped off her shoes and sat down on the sofa sleeper's mattress.

He shook his head. "It doesn't matter who they're playing. It's the Rangers. I always watch their games."

"I would have thought you were more of a football fan," she said, arranging pillows behind her. "You were Royal High School's star running back and played varsity all four years." She paused as she thought back on their high school days. "And didn't you play in college?"

"Yup, I went to Texas State on a football scholarship. It's my favorite, but I played just about every sport Royal High had to offer," he said, nodding. "I was on the baseball team all four years, as well."

"I probably didn't notice because I was in dance class and always had practice for our spring dance recitals," she said, leaning back against the pillows.

"That's not surprising," he said, folding his arms behind his head. "You move like a dancer."

"You watch me move?" she asked, suddenly feeling a little self-conscious.

He turned his head to look over at her. "Sweetheart, I've always watched the way you move."

"Even when we were in school?" If the look in his

eyes was any indication, he must have liked what he'd observed.

"Actually, it was one of the first things I noticed about you the day I saw you coming down the hall toward me," he said, smiling. "You were wearing blue jeans and a green sweater that made your hair look a little more red than auburn."

She couldn't believe he had remembered so many details, but that wasn't what she'd been wearing the first day they'd met. "I probably wore that sweater another time. But the first day we met, I had on a peach-colored shirt and khaki slacks."

His slow smile sent a shiver of anticipation up her spine. "I didn't say it was the first day we met. I said it was the first time I saw you walking down the hall. It took me a couple of weeks after that to work up the nerve to introduce myself."

She couldn't believe Cole Richardson—the school jock and heartthrob of the Royal High School senior class—had been nervous about talking to a lowly sophomore girl, who was almost as flat-chested and taller than most of the boys her age. "I had no idea," she said, completely stunned by the revelation. "Why on earth were you nervous about talking to me?"

"Probably because I thought you were the prettiest girl I'd ever seen," he admitted. "And I wanted to ask you out. But I was afraid a girl as pretty as you would turn me down flat."

"But I wasn't allowed to date, as you found out," she said, wishing her parents hadn't been so strict. Maybe if they had allowed her to date at a younger age, she and Cole would have been high school sweethearts and her life would have turned out differently.

Cole shook his head. "Your parents were probably right about that. Although I had the best of intentions, I was still a teenage boy with more hormones than good sense. And no matter what guys say, at eighteen that's about all a boy has on his mind."

Deciding there was no better time, she asked him the question she had wondered about for more than ten years. "Why didn't you ask me out after I graduated like you said you would, Cole?"

He stared at her for several long seconds before he sighed heavily. "I had to take some classes that summer, Paige." He unfolded his arms and reached over to touch her cheek with his index finger. "Believe me, it was the last thing I wanted to do. But it was the only chance I had."

"I thought you had forgotten," she said, her skin tingling from the contact.

"No, I couldn't forget you," he said, pulling her over to rest her head on his shoulder. "After my classes were over, I had football practice and the season started."

"And I had started dating Craig," she said, unable to keep the resignation from her voice.

"Things don't always work out the way we plan," Cole said, wrapping his arms around her.

"No, they don't." She was supposed to have been happily married with two or three children by now. Instead, she was the childless widow of a man she hadn't loved.

"But sometimes, when you least expect it, we get a

do-over," Cole said, his tone philosophical. "We just have to be brave enough to take those second chances when they come along."

Was Cole telling her he wanted that for them? Or was he asking her if she had the courage to try?

Unsure, she remained silent as they settled back to watch the baseball game. She didn't want to assume too much or read something into his statement simply because she wanted it to be there. She also needed to decide if she wanted to enter into a relationship so soon after Craig's death. It had only been a little more than six months since that fateful day. Also, for the first time in her life, she was on her own. She was just beginning to realize her potential and who she was as a woman. And it felt good.

She yawned and closed her eyes as she snuggled closer to the man holding her to him. Was she willing to give up her newfound independence? Would Cole even want her to? Did he feel threatened by a woman's independence the way Craig seemed to have been?

Paige wasn't sure. Hopefully she would be able to think things through and find answers to her concerns before Cole left to go back to Dallas. She had a feeling that if they missed their opportunity to explore their feelings this time, there might not be another one.

Seven

When Cole woke up sometime after midnight, several things immediately became apparent. The baseball game had been over hours ago, Paige was sound asleep in his arms and he wanted her. Hell, if the truth were known, he'd wanted her since he'd returned to Royal over six months ago.

Unable to stop himself, he turned his head to place his mouth over hers. He told himself he was just going to give her a little good-night kiss and that would be it. But when her lips clung to his, he didn't even try to stop himself from continuing, nor did he consider that he was playing with a fire he might not be able to put out.

Soft and sweet, he traced her with his tongue as he savored the taste of her. Parting her lips on a contented sigh, Paige murmured his name and a surge of heat made a beeline straight to his lower body.

Deciding that he'd better call a halt to the caress before things went further than he intended, Cole moved to break the kiss. But it appeared that Paige had awakened with other ideas.

When she brought her delicate hand up to cup his cheek, her eyes locked with his. Cole could see the desire in the dark gray depths, and he felt as though he might go up in a puff of smoke right then and there. If he was reading her right, Paige wanted his kiss and a whole lot more. He couldn't have denied her if his life depended on it.

Bringing his mouth back down on hers, Cole deepened the caress to explore her thoroughly and completely. To his amazement, she kissed him back with the same degree of passion and need. His heart pounded hard in his chest when she engaged him in a game of advance and retreat, nipping at his lower lip with her teeth.

Some men might have found her taking control to be a threat to their masculinity. Cole found it sexy as hell. He was secure enough not to be intimidated and loved the fact that she wasn't afraid to show him what she wanted. He had a feeling that Paige was just beginning to discover her strength as a woman, and he wanted to be the man who helped her find it.

When he eased away from the kiss, he ran his fingers through her silky auburn hair as he rained tiny kisses along her delicate jaw and down her throat to her collarbone. "Paige, I want you." He raised his head to gaze down at her. "I want you to take me deep inside you and make me feel like you're never going to let me go. But if that isn't what you're feeling, too, tell me now."

"I want you, too," she said, nodding.

"Are you sure?" He kissed her cheeks, her eyes and the tip of her nose. "Because I don't want any awkwardness between us in the morning and no feelings of guilt. My making love with you this time won't be a way to escape the fear of a storm, it won't be a mistake, nor will it be disrespectful to Craig or your marriage to him. It will be just you and me sharing a special moment together."

"I've never wanted anything more in my life than to share that with you, Cole," she said without hesitation. "But what about your knee?"

He smiled as he lowered his head to brush his lips over the satiny skin along the column of her neck. "We'll have to be a little more creative. You can take the lead this time and be on top," he whispered.

"I've never been…on top," she said, running her hand down his side to the tail of his T-shirt.

Cole really wasn't surprised by her admission. His brother had been a very selfish individual and hadn't cared enough to encourage Paige's adventurous nature. But Cole wasn't going to think about it now. There would be plenty of time for that later. Right now, he had the most exciting woman in the entire world in his arms and he was determined to bring her as much pleasure as possible.

"You'll do just fine, Paige."

When she lifted his shirt to run her hands over his abdomen, he quickly pulled it over his head and tossed it to the floor. As she continued to explore his pectoral muscles and abs, a wave of heat flowed through his veins, making him a little light-headed.

"That feels…good," he said, groaning.

"I love your body," she said reverently. "I love touching you and learning what you like."

"Part of the excitement of making love is trying new things and finding new ways to give each other pleasure," he said as he unbuttoned the top of her polo shirt.

Lifting the garment over her head, he tossed it to the side as he reached for the front clasp of her lace bra. He made quick work of helping her out of it, then tossed it to the floor with their shirts. He held her gaze with his as he slowly covered one beautiful breast with his hand.

"You're perfect," he said as he gently touched her tight nipple with his thumb.

Cole reveled in the growing spark of desire in her pretty gray eyes. Lowering his head, he kissed the tip of her other breast, and then took the peak into his mouth. As he explored and teased her with his mouth and hand, he loved hearing a tiny moan escape her parted lips, loved the glow of excitement coloring her porcelain cheeks.

Slowly sliding his hand down her smooth flat stomach to the waistband of her jeans, he worked the button through the opening and eased the zipper down. As he captured her mouth with his, Cole slipped his fingers beneath the elastic band of her silk panties and parted her, stroking her with infinite care.

"Y-you're driving…me…crazy," she gasped.

"The good kind of crazy?" he asked as he smiled down at her.

"That…depends," she said breathlessly as she caressed his chest.

"What does it depend on, Paige?" he asked, continuing his tender assault.

"On what you intend to do about it," she said, closing her eyes for a moment as if savoring the sensations he was creating inside her. When she opened them, the passion he detected in her gray gaze robbed him of breath. "If you don't do something soon, I think I'll go completely insane."

"Then let's get the rest of these clothes off," he suggested.

Between kisses, they helped each other finish undressing, and by the time he took her back in his arms, Cole felt as if he would go up in a blaze of glory. Her soft form pressed to his harder flesh caused him to feel as if he had been branded. Burning to make her his again, he had to take several deep breaths to slow down the fever building inside him.

"I need to love you now, Paige," he said, feeling as if he was close to losing the slender hold he had on his control. "Straddle my hips, sweetheart."

When she did, her smile was replaced by a look of pure ecstasy as she took him in. "I feel so…complete," she murmured, closing her eyes.

He tried to slow himself down, but his body was urging him to complete the act of making love to her. "You feel so damned good." Gritting his teeth, he struggled to hold himself in check. "I don't want to rush you, but I want you more than my next breath."

Placing his hands on her hips, he guided her into a slow rocking motion. No other woman had ever held him as tightly or as perfectly as Paige. Somehow he knew as surely as he knew his own name that no other woman ever would.

As the heat running through his veins began to gather in his loins, Cole felt Paige's tiny feminine muscles tighten around him and knew she was close to finding her satisfaction. Touching her where their bodies joined, he gently stroked her and watched as she slipped over the edge. Her release triggered his own, and he held her to him as waves of pleasure coursed through both of them.

When she collapsed on top of him, Cole stroked her long auburn hair and held her close. Now that he knew the truth about Craig and how uncaring he had been with Paige, Cole didn't feel a bit of remorse for making love with her. He cherished her as his brother never had and he saw no reason to suppress his attraction to her any longer.

He was pretty sure she felt the same way. Otherwise she wouldn't have made love with him. But he wasn't going to rush things between them, even though Paige was everything he'd ever wanted. He needed to make sure she was as comfortable with her feelings as he was with his.

Besides, he had a few things to get lined up with R&N Builders before they went any further. He and Aaron had talked about opening a satellite office in

Royal after Aaron and Stella got married. But they needed to have a serious talk about the future of their business if both he and Aaron remained in the area.

"That was beautiful," Paige said, raising her head to look down at him.

Deciding to push thoughts of R&N Builders future to the back burner, Cole kissed her chin. "You're beautiful."

When she moved to his side, Cole gathered her to him and covered them with the sheet. For a man who had never cared to share his bed for an entire night with a woman, he found that doing so with Paige felt like the most natural thing in the world.

As she snuggled against him, he closed his eyes and enjoyed the feeling of her lying against him. But a sudden thought had him opening his eyes to stare at the ceiling and kept him awake long after Paige drifted off to sleep.

What if he had gotten her pregnant?

Both times they'd made love, he had failed to use protection. The first time, they had both been distracted by the storm. It was a weak excuse, but he had taken Paige at her word that she didn't think she could become pregnant.

Tonight was an entirely different story. He could understand Paige dismissing the issue. But after reading Craig's emails, he knew the real reason she was childless and it had nothing whatsoever to do with infertility. Craig had purposely avoided having children with her by avoiding the fertile days of her cycle because when the time came, he had wanted to be able to make a clean break from her.

But Cole had known the truth and had ignored his responsibility of using protection. Was he looking to become a daddy? Just because Paige's first pregnancy had ended with a miscarriage didn't mean that another pregnancy wouldn't be successful.

Glancing down at the sleeping woman in his arms, he tried to imagine what it would be like to see Paige pregnant with their baby. With her inherent need to take care of her family, she would be a wonderful mother, and he would like nothing more than to give her the babies she had always wanted.

But she should be aware that it was a possibility and have a choice in the matter. He couldn't in good conscience continue to make love to her without using some kind of protection. It was one thing for him to know the reason behind her failure to conceive. But she had no idea about Craig's deception, and telling her would require Cole to explain how he knew why she had remained childless for the past ten years. As far as he was concerned that wasn't even on the table for consideration. He couldn't bear to see the devastation on her pretty face when she learned how little she'd meant to his brother or the cruelty of Craig letting her believe she was unable to have children.

As he felt sleep begin to overtake him, Cole knew his decision had been made. He was going to protect Paige from learning the truth for two simple reasons. For one thing, her knowing what his brother had done wouldn't change anything and would only add disillusionment to the emotional pain she had already suffered. And for another, dragging Craig's name through the mud and exposing him for the narcissistic sociopath that he was would make Cole no better than his twin had been.

After Cole's doctor's appointment on Thursday, Paige stood in the paint aisle of the Royal lumberyard and hardware store comparing colors. "Cole, what do you think of this color?" she asked. "I really like the warm cream, but white or off white might reflect the light a little better."

"Colors that reflect light are more your area of expertise than they are mine," Cole answered, looking over her shoulder at the samples she held. "Why don't you just go with the color you like best? I doubt there would be that much difference in the amount of light they reflect."

"You're probably right," she said, deciding on the warm cream color. "I'm probably overthinking things."

"Hey," he said, turning her to face him. "It's your studio and you should have whatever you want."

His smile warmed her all the way to her toes as he lowered his head for a kiss. His lips moved over hers with precision and care, and even though the caress was rather chaste, she felt a little breathless by the time he lifted his head.

"You're going to get us kicked out of the lumberyard," she said, laughing as she looked up and down the aisle to see if anyone had witnessed the kiss.

Cole laughed. "As long as R&N Builders keeps buying our supplies from them, I'm pretty sure they'll turn a blind eye."

She could tell Cole was a lot happier than he had been for the past week. At his appointment this afternoon, the orthopedist had removed the large bandage covering his knee and he was now allowed to put partial weight on that leg. He still had to use the crutches, but it was much easier to steady himself as he walked. He also seemed to be happier now that they were browsing the aisles at the lumberyard than he'd seemed when they had stopped at the grocery store earlier. She supposed it was a guy thing, but he had definitely shown more interest in the cabinetry they'd looked at for her studio than he had in the broccoli and cauliflower she had selected in the grocery store's produce section.

"How does your leg feel?" she asked, realizing how long he'd been moving around on it.

"It's a little sore but nothing I can't handle," he said, repeating the same thing he told her every time she asked.

"I'm definitely going with the cream color," she said, handing him the sample. They had already picked out floor tile and her cabinets and with the selection of the paint she was almost certain they had everything for her studio.

"I'll put these on the list for R&N's next delivery for the Double R build," he said, putting the paint chip in his shirt pocket.

"Is there anything else I need to pick out before we

head back home?" she asked as they started toward the courtesy desk.

He looked thoughtful. "I can't think of anything here. But I do need to stop by the pharmacy."

She waited for Cole to give the store clerk a list of items to be added to the next delivery for the ranch. "Did the doctor give you another prescription to have filled?" she asked as they walked out of the store.

"No, I'm going to buy a box of condoms," he whispered close to her ear.

"But why?" she asked, frowning in puzzlement. "I told you that I don't think I'm able to get pregnant."

"And there's the key word," he said as they got into her Mercedes. "You don't *think* it's possible. But you don't know for sure."

"Well, no, I haven't had my suspicion confirmed by a doctor, but I haven't become pregnant in ten years," she said, a little less certain than she'd been a few minutes ago.

"Did you ever stop to think it might be Craig's fault?" Cole asked.

She shook her head. "If you'll remember he made me pregnant before we got married and I haven't been able to become pregnant since. That suggests that it might be my problem. I might not be able to sustain a pregnancy."

To her surprise, Cole shook his head. "It doesn't matter. Men can become sterile at any time and for a variety of reasons." He reached over to take her hand in his. "I just don't want to make you pregnant until that's what you want."

Her heart skipped a beat. It was something she hadn't considered, and she had to admit he had a valid point. But it was the way he explained his reasons for buying the protection that stopped her in her tracks. He didn't want to make her pregnant until she wanted him to? Did that mean he was all right with them having a baby?

Paige gave herself a mental shake. She always seemed to be reading things into what Cole said and it was past time she stopped. Men had a habit of phrasing things differently than women and their intentions weren't always what women perceived them to be.

"All right," she said, putting the sedan into Drive. "Next stop, the pharmacy and then home."

A few minutes later, while Cole went into the pharmacy, Paige waited outside in the car at his request. He didn't give her a reason, but she had a feeling he might think she would be embarrassed at the checkout when all they purchased was a box of condoms.

"That was quick," she said when he slid back into the passenger seat a few minutes later.

"A lot of men won't admit it, but they have a size and brand they prefer," Cole said, grinning.

"I thought those were a one-size-fits-all kind of item," she said, laughing.

Cole laughed with her. "Sweetheart, contrary to the observations of our country's founding fathers, all men *are not* created equal."

As their laughter faded, they each fell silent, and Paige couldn't help but marvel at how easy it was to be with Cole. They both liked many of the same things, they enjoyed rooting for the Rangers baseball team and their sense of humor was similar.

"Are we still on for our date tonight?" Cole asked as Paige steered the car up the lane leading to the ranch house.

"Date?" She shook her head. "I have no idea what you're talking about."

"You, me, propped up on the sofa bed with the Rangers playing the Yankees." His wide grin faded. "I figure it will be one of our last nights in the family room now that I'm able to move around a little easier and will be able to get upstairs to my room soon."

She nodded as she parked the car in the garage. "You're probably right. The physical therapist will be here again tomorrow afternoon."

"Yeah, and results are pretty quick. I'm amazed after each session at the progress I've made," he said as they got out of the car and went into the house. "And that's just fine with me. I'd like to get back to work."

"But you've been overseeing things from the lawn chair under the tree for the past several days," she reminded him.

"Yeah, but that isn't all that I normally do," he said. "I like to inspect things, and that requires climbing ladders and making sure the job is done right."

"You don't trust your men?" she asked as they walked through the mud room.

"I do trust them, but—"

"You like doing some of the work yourself," she guessed.

He grinned. "Well, there is that."

When they entered the kitchen, Paige looked at the clock. "I think I better start dinner." Turning, she caught Cole wincing. "And you had better stretch out for a while and elevate your knee."

He gave her a short nod. "I might have been on it a little too long today."

"Do you need my help getting your leg propped up?" she asked, taking a casserole dish from the cabinet.

"No, I think I can manage to stuff a couple of pillows under it," he said as he continued on down the hall.

Two hours later, after she watched Cole devour the steak-and-potato casserole she had made for dinner and a huge slice of chocolate cake for dessert, she cleaned the kitchen and started the dishwasher while he went to turn on the baseball game. But entering the family room for their date to watch the baseball game, she stopped short when she saw how busy he'd been. There were several candles lit on the mantel, and he had propped up pillows for her to lean back against when she stretched out beside him. And he was sound asleep.

Smiling, she went around the room blowing out the candles, then went upstairs to change into her night-shirt. Cole had to be exhausted from being on his feet for several hours and if he was able to escape some of the lingering discomfort in his knee by going to sleep, she wasn't going to wake him.

When she finished changing, she went back down-stairs to the family room. Pulling the sheet back, she got into the bed beside him. She snuggled close and smiled when he pulled her into his arms and held her to him in his sleep.

At the age of nineteen, she'd envisioned her marriage might one day be this way. Unfortunately, after she'd gotten married and moved to the Double R she had never been able to see Craig as the loving husband in those daydreams.

Paige sighed as she felt herself start to drift off to sleep. She hadn't loved Craig, and he hadn't loved her. She had accepted that. But it hadn't kept her from hoping that one day he would give her a reason to care as deeply for him as she had always cared for Cole—the way she still did.

"What time will your meeting be over?" Cole asked as he and Paige walked through the doors of the Texas Cattleman's Club the following week.

The physical therapy had worked wonders, and he was down to using a cane. The therapist had assured him that by the middle of next week, he would probably be able to do without that as long as he took it easy and didn't try to rush his progress. And that suited him just fine. He was more than ready to get back to work full-time, even if it was with a few restrictions for a while.

"I'll give the program on the charity's mission to the new volunteers, then we'll break for brunch and have the business meeting after that," she said, sounding distracted as she checked her tote bag for at least the tenth time since they'd left the ranch. "It will probably be early afternoon by the time everything is over."

Cole put his hands on her shoulders and gazed

down into her amazing gray eyes. "Stop worrying. Your notes for the program are still in the tote bag, the same as they were the other nine times you checked." He kissed her forehead. "Relax. You're going to do just fine, sweetheart."

"What about you?" she asked. "How long do you think your meeting with Aaron will take? I hate to think you'll just be sitting around waiting on me."

"You're fussing again," he said, laughing.

She smiled. "I'll have to work on that."

He shook his head. "Don't work on it too hard. I kind of like having you fuss over me." He smiled. "Aaron and I are going to discuss plans for the new branch office and a couple of other ideas I've been mulling over. After that we're meeting Luc for lunch. I'm sure by the time your meeting is over, I'll be ready to go."

She took a deep breath. "I guess I'm as ready as I'll ever be, then."

"You look beautiful, you've got all your notes ready and you'll blow the socks off all those women," he assured her.

"Hey, you two," Aaron greeted them as he entered the clubhouse. "Cole, it's good to see you up and on your feet again instead of lying in a hospital bed with a goofy grin on your face."

"Now you know how you looked that time you fell off that ladder and had to take pain medication for your twisted ankle," he shot back good-naturedly. "Or how about the time I had to take you to the ER because you—"

"Never mind," Aaron said, laughing. "I get it. We've

both got enough on each other to ensure the other's silence from here on out."

Cole grinned. "Just so we're clear on that."

"I hope you get a lot accomplished," Paige said, smiling at Aaron. Then she turned to Cole, and the smile she gave him sent his temperature soaring. "I'll see you after my meeting."

He barely resisted the urge to take her in his arms. "We'll be in the club's sports bar."

As he watched her walk away, Aaron elbowed him in the ribs. "And you said I had it bad when I had my shorts in a bunch over Stella."

"Shut up, Nichols," Cole said, grinning.

Aaron laughed and started down the hall toward the meeting rooms. "I've reserved a private meeting room for us."

Cole nodded. "Good. I've got a new idea to run past you and I'd like to keep it on the down low for the time being."

As they entered and sat down at a small conference table, a door at the other end of the room opened and a waiter quietly carried over a tray with a carafe of coffee, cups and a platter of pastries. "If you need anything else, please let me know," the man said before turning to leave the room.

"Okay, what do you want to talk over first?" Aaron asked, pouring them both a cup of coffee.

"I know we agreed that we'd open an R&N satellite office here in Royal, but what do you think of moving the main part of the business down here and having the satellite office in Dallas?" Cole asked.

His coffee cup halfway to his mouth, Aaron stopped to stare at Cole. "Oh, man, you're in as deep as I am, aren't you?"

Cole didn't try to pretend he didn't know what his friend meant. "Paige is the girl I told you about having a crush on when we were in high school."

"But she married your brother," Aaron said, finally taking a sip of his coffee.

"It's a long story and maybe one day I'll tell you all about it," Cole said, unwilling to go into the details of his twin's character flaws.

He had never told anyone what had transpired between Craig and him ten years ago. Aaron knew there had been bad blood between them, but he didn't know why they'd had a falling out. For the time being, Cole wanted to keep it that way. He knew Aaron would understand. Aaron had had to conquer a few demons of his own before he'd been able to share the details of his first wife's and child's deaths in a car accident several years ago.

"You're thinking you might want to move back to Royal now that Paige is single again?" Aaron asked.

"Yeah, I do," Cole said, nodding. "Royal is my hometown and I've been away a long time. I've missed it."

"You mean you've missed a pretty auburn-haired rancher," Aaron said, grinning.

Instead of answering, Cole just smiled and sipped his coffee.

"So what does the lady have to say about it?" Aaron asked, sitting back in his chair.

"I haven't mentioned it to her yet," Cole admitted. "I wanted to talk to you first since it's a business decision we both need to agree on."

"I appreciate that," Aaron said, nodding. "But I'm good with moving the main office down here. This is where my life is now."

"That's probably because you're married to the mayor and expecting a baby in a couple of months," Cole said, laughing.

Aaron gave him a sheepish grin. "Well, yeah. That has a lot to do with it."

They fell silent for a moment before Cole finally admitted, "It would help if I knew how Paige felt about me being around all of the time." He set his empty coffee cup on the tray. "I'm pretty sure she wants that, but we haven't talked about it."

Grinning like a Cheshire cat, Aaron pointed to Cole's neck. "Yeah, if that little love bite you're sporting on the side of your neck is any indication, you haven't been doing a lot of talking at all."

Cole should have known Aaron would notice. It was just a tiny mark, but the man had the eyes of a hawk.

"Remind me again why we're friends and business partners," Cole said, scowling at his best friend.

Aaron laughed. "Damned if I know."

"If you're agreeable, we can keep the Dallas office open," Cole said, getting back to their discussion. "We could promote Jim Edwards to office manager. He's our best foreman and has been with us from the beginning. He knows the business inside and out and won't have any problem overseeing the projects and bringing in new business. You and I could take turns going up there once a month to check on things, and there's always internet meetings and telecommuting."

"That sounds good to me," Aaron agreed. "We've got enough builds lined up down here, we can put quite a few people to work right away, as well as keep everyone working up there."

"It sounds like we have a plan," Cole said, sticking his hand out to seal the deal.

Aaron shook his hand and stood up. "Now, let's go meet Luc for lunch and toast moving the business to Royal with a beer."

As he and his partner left the meeting room, Cole smiled. He had one more thing left to do and one more stamp of approval to make his plans complete. He needed to talk to Paige and find out if she was open to having him hang around indefinitely.

Eight

The following Monday morning as she made breakfast, Paige felt happier than she had in years. She and Cole had spent a wonderful weekend together. On Saturday afternoon, he had insisted they take a drive around the ranch for him to show her some of his favorite places to play when he'd been a young boy. She had enjoyed seeing his favorite fishing spot along the creek and hearing his story about falling in when he was ten years old and thinking he would drown until he figured out he could stand up and the water only came up to his waist. They had also seen some of the big live oaks and cottonwoods that the tornado had uprooted as it made its way across the land.

Then when they had returned to the house, he had grilled steaks and vegetables for dinner before they cuddled on the sofa in the family room to watch the baseball game. It was a glimpse of the way their life could have been and the way she hoped life would be for them in the future.

He had mentioned that he had something he needed to discuss with her, but they never seemed to get around to it. She smiled when she thought about the reasons why they hadn't talked. It seemed that they couldn't be in the same room for more than five minutes without having their arms around each other.

She briefly wondered if he wanted to talk about the future. They hadn't discussed what would happen when he and his construction crew finished the barn and the repairs to the outbuildings, but she was hoping they could work out something. His life was in Dallas and hers was on the Double R, but surely they could find a way to spend time together. Maybe he could come down to Royal one weekend and she could travel up to Dallas the next.

"Uh-oh," Cole said, entering the kitchen and walking over to where she stood at the counter cracking eggs to scramble for breakfast.

Looking over her shoulder at him, she smiled. "You didn't want eggs?"

"No, the eggs are fine," he said, grinning. Standing behind her, he wrapped his arms around her waist to pull her back against him. "I've seen that look before. What are you worrying about this time?"

"What I'm going to make for dinner tonight," she fibbed.

He had a work crew arriving soon and she didn't

want to get into a discussion about what the future might hold for them. That subject should be broached when they had plenty of time to talk about what they both wanted and where they felt their feelings for each other were leading them.

"As far as I'm concerned, I'd be happy having you," he whispered close to her ear.

A shiver of anticipation coursed through her. Since their talk the first morning they had awoken in each other's arms, they'd spent every night making love, holding each other while they slept and rising in the morning to greet the day together. And Paige had loved every minute of it.

"You're insatiable, Cole Richardson," she said, hoping he never changed.

"I can't help it," he said, turning her in his arms for a kiss that caused her knees to wobble. "You're amazing and I can't get enough of you."

She felt the same way about him, but his work crew chose that moment to drive up the lane to start work on the barn interior, so she decided to wait until later to tell him so. "It appears that we'll have to talk about your…appetite a bit later."

He groaned. "Duty calls." He kissed her soundly, walked to the back door and smiled as he took his wide-brimmed hat from the peg. "With any luck, we'll get the barn finished and start repairing the equipment shed before we break for lunch."

"Don't try to do too much," she reminded him. "Remember what the doctor said about—"

"There you go fussing again," he said, laughing as he opened the door. "But I promise I won't overdo it."

Turning the scrambled eggs she had planned for Cole's breakfast into an omelet, Paige only managed to eat a few bites before the queasiness that had plagued her for the past few mornings set in. Scraping the rest of the food into the garbage disposal, she frowned. What was wrong with her? Beyond an occasional head cold, she was normally very healthy and she never lost her appetite.

But as she stood there wondering if she was coming down with some type of stomach flu, a sudden thought had her rushing into the office to look at her personal calendar. After checking the dates three times, she sat back in the desk chair in disbelief. She was almost two weeks late. The only other time that had happened was when she had become pregnant before she got married.

Glancing down at her stomach, she shook her head. She was normally as regular as clockwork. Could she be pregnant again?

A mixture of emotion flowed through her at the thought. She had wanted a baby for so long, she was afraid to hope. What if she were pregnant? How would Cole take that kind of news?

"Stop it," she said out loud, forcing herself to be realistic.

She didn't know anything for certain and there was no sense in going over all the what-ifs until she did. Nibbling her lower lip, she decided there was only one way to find out.

Her hands trembled slightly as she dug through her

purse for her car keys, closed the door, got in her car and drove the five miles into Royal. Try as she might, she couldn't tamp down the nervous excitement as she drove straight to the pharmacy where Cole had purchased the condoms, bought the pregnancy test and drove right back home.

Ten minutes after she returned to the ranch, Paige stared at the two white sticks in her hand. Both digital windows showed a positive result. She had bought one of the latest and, according to the pharmacist, most accurate home pregnancy tests on the market. She had even made sure the package had two test sticks just in case she did something wrong and needed an extra. When the first stick showed a definite positive, she repeated the test just to be sure. There was no doubt about it. According to the tests that boasted 99 percent accuracy, she was pregnant.

Placing her hand protectively over her flat stomach, tears of joy ran down her cheeks. She was finally going to have a baby. A baby fathered by the man she had loved since he'd first introduced himself to her all those years ago in the halls of Royal High School.

Her heart skipped a beat as she thought about her feelings for Cole. She had loved him almost from the moment she met him. Since his return to Royal, those feelings had intensified to where there was no longer any doubt in her mind about how she felt. She loved him with all of her heart and soul. And he seemed to care a great deal for her.

But how on earth was she going to tell him she was pregnant? And how would he react?

He had said when he bought the condoms that he didn't want to make her pregnant until that was what she wanted. Did that mean he would be happy to have a baby with her? When should she tell him? And what was she going to say?

She couldn't very well throw that kind of news at him during an ordinary dinner conversation. Something like "the rain stopped early today and oh, by the way, I'm pregnant, and please pass the mashed potatoes" would never do. No, she needed to come up with the perfect way to tell Cole he was going to be a daddy.

Unable to figure out any answers, she decided to do the one thing that usually helped her think and work through whatever decisions she needed to make. Paige started cleaning.

Starting upstairs in her room, she cleaned the already tidy space, gathered the clothes that needed laundering and put them into a basket. Going across the hall into Cole's room, she cleaned there, as well. When she was done, she emptied his hamper into the basket and headed downstairs.

As she sorted the clothes to put into the washer, something fell to the floor. Picking it up, she wondered which one of them had left a computer flash drive in their pocket. It might be Cole's, but she doubted it. It looked just like the one Craig had given her a few years ago to use as a backup for her charity programs. Although she didn't remember putting it in her pocket, it must be hers. She'd had hers out the day she'd made notes for her presentation to the volunteers of the TCC

Tornado Relief Fund. She probably had just forgotten she'd put it there.

As soon as she started the washer, she walked into the den, booted up her computer and stuck the device into the USB port. She wasn't trying to be nosy, but she wanted to be certain it was hers instead of Cole's. All she needed to do was check the file directory and she would know for sure which one of them it belonged to.

As she scanned the files, her breath caught and her heart began to pound when she realized the memory device had belonged to Craig. She opened the first file, titled "My Marriage." It appeared to be a journal Craig had been keeping from shortly after they had gotten married until his death almost seven months ago. As she read the first entry tears pooled in her eyes. It made her realize how much he'd blamed her for his life turning out the way it had. He had resented his father making him marry her and had even written that he wished she'd had the miscarriage before the wedding instead of a few weeks later. If she had, he wouldn't have had to go through with their marriage at all.

As she read more and more of the files, it got worse. He talked about purposely avoiding making her pregnant by keeping track of her most fertile times of the month and avoiding lovemaking because the last thing he wanted was a brat to tie him to her even more so than he already was. In another one of the files he even seemed to find it humorous that he had been able to get her to move out of the master bedroom on the pretense of his being a restless sleeper.

All that time Craig had known how badly she had

wanted to have a baby and how sad she'd been when she hadn't become pregnant. He had even convinced her that she was infertile by pointing out that he had made her pregnant once and the miscarriage she suffered might be her body's inability to support a pregnancy. How could he have done that to her? And why had she listened to him?

As she continued going through the directory, Paige found file after file filled with intense blame and loathing for her and how she had ruined his life. Craig had also written extensively about his "business trips" and how convenient it had been that his father's health had started failing and how it had kept her busy taking care of the old man while Craig took his current mistress to a new spa or on a weeklong gambling junket to Las Vegas. After an hour of reading about his illicit escapades with other women, Paige lost count of how many affairs Craig had had over the years.

As she sat there staring at the computer screen, she had to admit that she'd wondered about his frequent out-of-town trips. Maybe if she had cared more for him she would have questioned him about them. But she hadn't, and if she were perfectly honest, she had been happy for some time to herself and hadn't minded his being gone all that much. Unable to read any more of the sickening passages, she started to exit out of the directory, but Cole's name at the bottom of the list caught her eye. Why did Craig have a file with Cole's name on it?

Clicking it open, she realized that Craig had been corresponding with Cole for the past couple of years.

She frowned. That couldn't be right. Cole had made it clear that he hadn't had anything to do with Craig since leaving for college.

Why hadn't Cole mentioned the email Craig had sent to him? And why had Craig saved the messages?

Unwilling to read more of Craig's disgusting thoughts than she had to, she only opened a couple of the documents. As she read the last one, her heart sank and by the time she finished, Paige felt as if the world had suddenly spun out of control as she read Craig's ramblings. He was telling Cole that he intended to leave her for another woman and that Cole could finally have his turn with her because Craig was done and moving on.

"Oh, my God!" she gasped.

How could she have been so gullible? Why hadn't she seen through Craig's deception and lies?

But of all the revelations, the one that shattered her heart into a million pieces was the realization that Cole had known what Craig had been doing and the hurtful things he had said about her. Tears poured down her cheeks as she thought about the last line of Craig's email. "Now that I'm done with her, you can finally have your turn with Paige."

Had she been a pawn in a sick game the twin brothers had been playing all these years? How could they do that to her? What had she ever done to them to make them want to ruin her life?

Her stomach lurched and she had to run for the downstairs powder room to be sick. She had married one brother because she was pregnant, and now she was pregnant with the other brother's baby. It appeared that history was repeating itself.

But she wasn't going to be trapped in another depraved game with another Richardson brother. Once was enough to last her an entire lifetime and then some.

As soon as she managed to compose herself, she had every intention of ordering Cole to pack his things and leave the ranch. After what he and Craig had done to her, the way they had manipulated her life, she didn't care that the Double R had been in his family for years. It was hers now and if he ever dared to step foot on the property again, she would have him arrested for trespassing.

When Cole entered the house, he expected to find Paige in the kitchen making sandwiches for him and the work crew to have for lunch. She was nowhere in sight. She wasn't in the family room or the room she wanted to turn into her studio, either.

"Paige," he called as he walked through the house.

When she wasn't in the den, he climbed the stairs and finally found her sitting on the side of the bed in his room. Her head was slightly tilted down as if she was studying her hands, which were twisted into a tight knot in her lap.

"Why didn't you answer me?" When she lifted her eyes to look at him, the abject pain in the crystalline gray depths made him feel as if he'd taken a head butt to the gut.

"Paige, sweetheart, what's wrong?" he demanded,

crossing the room to stand in front of her. When he reached for her hands, she jerked them away.

"Don't call me that," she said, her voice tense with emotion. "And I don't want you ever to touch me again."

Sensing that whatever had happened was going to take a lot longer to resolve than just his lunch hour, Cole turned to leave the room. "I'll be right back."

As he went downstairs, he took his billfold out of the hip pocket of his jeans and removed a couple of hundred dollar bills. Stepping outside, he called to Harold. When the man reached the porch, Cole handed him the money. "Take the crew to the Royal Diner for lunch on me, then everyone has the rest of the day off with pay."

Without waiting for the man to comment, Cole walked back into the house, closed the door and retraced his steps back upstairs to his room. "Now, why don't you tell me what's going on?" he asked, walking over to the bed.

When he sat down beside Paige, she rose to her feet and walked several paces away. "I want you off the ranch as soon as you can pack your things." She turned back to face him. "And I don't ever want you to come back. If you do, I swear I'll have Sheriff Battle arrest you."

"Do you mind telling me what I've done?" he asked calmly. If she knew him better, she would realize his demeanor was a facade he had perfected years ago to keep his brother from knowing just how much he was getting to him.

"I'm not going to go into everything," she said,

shaking her head. "It's too sordid to repeat. But I know what you and Craig were up to and the sick game you were playing at my expense. It was your turn to have me? Really, Cole? How could you?"

Cole's heart came to a complete halt. Without thinking, he asked, "How did you find out?"

He watched her close her eyes a moment as if she were struggling to maintain her composure. "Oh, dear Lord, Cole, does it matter?" Opening her eyes, she stared at him. "How I found out isn't important. I told you I know about your vile game and that's all that matters. Now please pack your clothes, take your men and leave."

"Who's going to finish the barn and repairs to your other buildings?" he asked, stalling for time. He needed to think of a way to get her to listen to him. But at the moment, it appeared hell would freeze over before that happened.

"I'll hire someone else to do the work." She shook her head so vehemently that her ponytail swayed back and forth. "I want nothing more to do with you or your company."

Deciding that she needed time to cool down and he needed time to think, Cole got up from the bed and opened the closet to get his suitcase. "I can arrange to have Aaron take over the job. There's no sense penalizing the workers because you have a problem with me. Besides, the barn is almost finished and all that's left are the repairs to the sheds and turning that room into your studio."

"I'll think about it and let him know," she said,

walking to the door. "I want no further contact with you." Then she left the room.

As he gathered his things, Cole searched for the gym shorts he'd worn the day he discovered the memory stick with Craig's journal and copies of the messages he'd sent to Cole. He had put it in his pocket when Paige walked into the room that day to keep her from seeing the damning evidence of Craig's depravity. When he failed to find the shorts along with several other items of his clothing, he bet every dime he had that she'd been doing laundry and had found it.

Stuffing clothes into the suitcase, he cursed himself for being a damned fool. He had been so sure he could protect Paige from learning about the ugly side of Craig's personality that he had been careless. Now she thought he had known and been in on his brother's twisted escapades all along.

Cole stopped packing for a moment as a thought suddenly occurred to him. How could he possibly prove that he wasn't involved and had no knowledge of Craig's scheme?

He had deleted all of the messages from his own email account without reading them and, with the exception of their father's funeral, hadn't had any contact with his brother since he'd left home after their fight more than a decade ago. Unfortunately, he could talk until he lost his voice and Paige wasn't going to believe him. At least, not now. His only chance was to put distance between them and hope that when he returned in a day or two she would hear him out and believe what he told her.

After he carried his suitcase downstairs, he found her in the kitchen staring out the window above the sink. When she turned to face him, he could tell she had been crying. The knowledge damned near tore him apart.

"Paige, I—"

"Please don't, Cole," she said, holding up one hand to stop him when he started toward her. "I think it would be best if you just leave."

He wanted to take her in his arms and make all the emotional pain go away, but it was clear she wouldn't welcome the gesture. And once he touched her, he knew he'd never be able to let her go.

"Let me know if you need me for anything," he said as he walked to the back door.

"Not that you or your brother ever have, but don't worry about me," Paige said. "I'm a survivor. It may take me a while, but I'll be just fine on my own."

With nothing left that he could say to change her mind—at least for the time being—Cole walked out of the house, got into his truck and drove toward the outskirts of Royal. Although it didn't sit well, he couldn't honestly say he blamed her for not wanting to listen to anything a Richardson had to say. She had just learned that everything she thought she knew about her marriage and the past ten years of her life had been a complete lie. And even in death Craig was manipulating both of them and ruining their chances of being happy together.

Cole suddenly brought the truck to a screeching halt in the middle of the deserted highway. Paige must have only read the last email Craig had sent to him. She had talked about him and Craig playing her for the fool and she mentioned knowing that it was his turn with her. But if she had read all of the emails, she would have realized from the very first one that he had fought to try and stop Craig.

Paige was emotionally devastated and he had a way to put a stop to some of the hell she was going through. And that's exactly what he intended to do.

Knowing he had found the evidence to prove that he was in no way involved in anything Craig did, Cole turned the truck around and headed back to the Double R Ranch. He had loved Paige from the moment he'd laid eyes on her in the halls of Royal High School, and he was almost positive she had loved him just as long.

He had intended to tell her how he felt and ask her to marry him this past weekend. But they hadn't been able to keep their hands off each other, and he'd put it off in favor of getting a ring and planning something to make his proposal special. Unfortunately, that was no longer an option.

Cole pushed the gas pedal all the way to the floor and raced back to the only woman he had ever loved. He'd lost her once, but he'd be damned if he lost her again.

Nine

As she watched Cole walk out the door without a backward glance, Paige felt her heart break all over again. When she'd confronted him with what she had discovered on the flash drive, he hadn't tried to deny it. He'd only wanted to know how she'd found out about it.

She picked up a box of tissues, climbed the stairs, went into her bedroom and curled up into a tight ball on her bed. Cole's betrayal was without a doubt the most devastating thing she had ever experienced. Nothing in her entire life even came close to causing her the emotional pain she was feeling at that moment.

How could the utter joy of finding out she was going to have his baby be replaced so quickly by absolute desolation?

What Craig had done, the vile game he had played

to ruin her life, had been despicable. But it was nothing compared to Cole's duplicity. If she were completely honest with herself, she had always known that Craig was shallow and self-centered, and on some level, she had even known there were other women. But she had completely believed in Cole's sincerity and that he truly cared for her.

How could she have been so wrong about him? Why had she allowed herself to believe he cared for her as deeply as she cared for him?

Clutching her pillow, she sobbed into it as she realized another one of her dreams had died at the hands of a Richardson brother. For ten years Craig had taken her hopes of having a family away from her. Then, just when she learned she was going to finally have a baby, Cole had shattered the dream that she would also have the love of a good man as they raised that child together.

"Paige?" She heard Cole call from downstairs.

Why hadn't he listened when she told him to go away and never come back? Was he so determined to destroy her life as it seemed his brother had done that he came back just to ensure he had accomplished his goal?

Before she could collect herself and get up from the bed to face off with him again, she heard his footsteps as he entered the room.

"Please don't cry, Paige," Cole said as his strong arms wrapped around her to lift her to him.

Lost in her misery, she hadn't had the strength to

move fast enough to evade him. "Turn me loose and leave or I'll—"

"Yeah, I know. You'll call Nathan Battle and have me arrested," he said, making no move to let her go. Nor did he sound all that concerned about his impending trip to jail.

"Why are you doing this, Cole?" she demanded, unable to stop the tears from rolling down her cheeks. "Haven't you humiliated me enough? What else do you want from me?"

"Paige, there's no reason to feel embarrassed or betrayed," he said, his tone as gentle as she'd ever heard. "All I want is for you to hear me out. I swear to you that what you think you know isn't what really happened."

"Please, just leave me alone, Cole." She hated that she couldn't stop crying. She didn't want him to see how badly he had hurt her.

"You need to listen to me," he insisted.

When she pushed against his wide chest, he finally released her. "Go away, Cole." She scrambled to the other side of the bed and out of his reach. "There's nothing you have to say that I want to hear."

"You have to know I would never hurt you, Paige," he said, his voice deceptively sincere.

"And just how would I know that?" she asked, her anger beginning to chase away a bit of her devastation. "Everything I thought I knew about you and your brother has turned out to be nothing but lies and deception."

"That might be true for Craig, but not for me," he said, shaking his head. "I've never lied to you, nor have I ever done anything that I thought would hurt you in any way."

"You've never lied to me?" she scoffed. "That's not the way I remember it."

He stubbornly shook his head. "If I've said something to you that wasn't true, it was completely unintentional."

With the evidence she had discovered, she had a hard time believing him. "Really, Cole? If I remember correctly, you've lied to me as long as I've known you."

"How do you figure that?" he asked, frowning.

"You promised that you were going to ask me out as soon as I graduated from high school." She shook her head. "We both know how that turned out."

"I'm sorry about that, Paige." Surprisingly, he still had the nerve to look her in the eyes. "I fully intended to do what I'd said. But I had good reason not to keep that promise."

Whatever it was, she didn't think she wanted to hear it. "I waited for you that entire summer and the only reason I finally went out with Craig was because I got tired of him asking all the time." From the expression on his handsome face, she could tell Cole was holding something back —something he wasn't telling her. "What was your reason, Cole?" she asked, deciding she did want to hear his lame excuse just before she kicked him out of her life for good. "And before you answer, keep in mind that I've had a lifetime of lies. I want the truth this time."

He took a deep breath and rubbed at the back of his neck. "I was trying to protect you from Craig."

"How on earth could you possibly think that by not asking me out you were protecting me from your brother?" she demanded.

Cole stared at her for endless seconds before he spoke again. "Let me tell you something about Craig you probably don't know. He had a mission in life and that was to try to make me miserable or to take anything away from me that I valued or cared for." He took a deep breath. "After we got out of high school, Craig found out that I had a crush on you and told me he intended to not only make you his girlfriend, he was going to take your virginity."

"Oh, my God!" Her breath caught on a sob as she thought of how cold and calculating Craig had been and how he had planned to ruin her life even before they married.

Cole stood up and began to pace the length of her bedroom as if it bothered him that he'd upset her. "That happened while I was home on spring break the year you graduated. The same week I broke Craig's nose."

Paige gasped. "The two of you fought over me?"

Cole shrugged. "It wasn't much of a fight. I told him to leave you alone. It pissed me off when he said no. So I stuck out my fist and he just happened to be closer than he should have been."

She shook her head. "I still don't see how you thought ignoring me was going to dissuade him."

"I had hoped that if he thought I'd lost interest in you, he would give up and leave you alone." Cole shook his head. "That's why I didn't ask you out and stayed away that entire summer."

She frowned. "You still haven't explained why you thought that tactic would work."

"Craig normally had the attention span of a flea," Cole answered. "As soon as he thought he had prevented me from having what I wanted, he moved on to trying to torture me with something else. Unfortunately, that was the one time it didn't work. Apparently, Craig saw through the ruse."

Cole looked as if he was being truthful with her. But she'd learned the hard way that appearances could be deceiving when it came to the Richardson brothers. And it was all so sordid, she had a hard time believing what he said.

"Why didn't you just tell me what he had planned?" she asked. "Wouldn't that have been simpler than playing head games with him?"

"You have to remember, a twenty-year-old isn't much more than a boy and doesn't normally have the reasoning skills of a thirty-year-old man. Besides, I didn't figure you would believe me," Cole admitted. "It's so damned twisted even I have a hard time believing how Craig's mind worked."

"You're probably right." She shook her head. "But I've seen the evidence. You knew what Craig was up to and were obviously in on Craig's scheme. In the email he said it was your turn to have me because he was done and intended to move on."

"Paige, you didn't read all of the messages, did you?" he asked.

"No. I only made it through a couple of them and they were more than enough to make me sick. Especially after reading Craig's journal." She shuddered just thinking about how vile his ramblings had been.

"That's what I thought." Cole walked over to stand in front of her. "If you had opened the first email in the file, you would have known about what I just told you. In it, Craig was gloating about the fight failing to dissuade him and how he had succeeded in ruining any chances I'd had with you. The rest of the emails outlined what his life had been like being married to you."

Tears filled her eyes as a thought suddenly occurred to her. "He started sending those emails almost two years ago. You've known all this time and you didn't tell me," she accused. "You must think I'm the biggest fool who ever lived."

"I've never thought that about you, Paige." Sitting down beside her, Cole shook his head. "And until I found that flash drive the day I went through those boxes from Craig's office, I didn't know anything that was in them. Apparently Craig hid it in the box with my trophies and probably intended to send it to me at some point in time."

"I can't believe that you didn't know anything about the messages," she stated flatly. "He sent those to you. You had to know what he was up to and the horrible things he said."

"I have no way to prove it, but I deleted every one of them unread," Cole answered.

"Not even one?" she asked, still skeptical.

He shook his head. "Not even one. I wasn't interested in anything Craig had to say." He gently took her hands in his. "Don't you see, Paige? We've both been victims in Craig's sick game for over ten years. And if we give up on what we've found together these past few weeks because of what he put in his journal and those messages, he's continuing to call the shots and make us victims—he wins again."

"What is it that you think we have together, Cole?" she asked, pulling her hands from his. Her faith had been shaken right down to the foundation and she wasn't certain of anything anymore.

"It's not what I think, sweetheart," he said, taking her into his arms. "It's what I know." When she started to push against his chest, the look in his incredible blue eyes stopped her. "I love you and I'm pretty damned sure you love me."

"You love me," she repeated. She had wanted to hear those words from Cole since she was sixteen years old, and now that he'd said them, she was having a hard time believing that she'd heard him correctly or that he meant them.

"Paige, I've loved you since I first I saw you walking toward me on your way to Mr. Matthews's geometry class," Cole said, holding her close. "You were the prettiest girl I'd ever seen. And that hasn't changed. If anything, you're more beautiful now than you were then."

He started to brush his lips over hers, but she turned her head slightly, causing him to kiss her cheek instead. "Cole, I don't want to be hurt again. I've recently discovered that in the past I've been too gullible and placed my trust too easily."

"I understand, sweetheart," he said, giving her a smile that curled her toes inside her cross-trainers. "But

I give you my word that everything I'm telling you is the truth. I love you more than life itself, and if you'll give me the chance, I swear I'll make sure no one ever hurts you again." He paused for a moment before he continued. "If you'll remember, I was able to tell you what you were wearing the first time I saw you, as well as the day I worked up the nerve to talk to you."

She nodded. "But what does that have to do with—?"

"To prove just how hard and fast I fell for you that day, I can tell you that your hair was pulled back from your face and clipped with two silver barrettes," he said, smiling. "And your backpack was purple with pink trim."

"How do you remember so many details about that day?" she asked, astounded that he recalled everything so accurately.

"Because I fell in love with you and didn't want to forget anything about you," he said as if it was as simple as that. "I never want to forget seeing the love of my life for the first time."

She bit her lower lip to keep it from trembling before she finally managed to get words passed the lump clogging her throat. "I think I've loved you just as long."

"Thank God!" He immediately brought his mouth down to cover hers with a kiss that left her breathless. When he raised his head, he brushed a tear from her cheek with his thumb as he stared into her eyes. "I never want you to doubt how much you mean to me. I'm going to spend every minute of every day for the rest of my life telling you how beautiful you are and how much I love you, Paige."

"And I love you, Cole," she said, knowing in her heart that everything he had told her was true.

He gave her a smile that took her breath away. "I wanted to wait until I had a ring and planned something special when I ask you, but I don't want to waste another minute. Will you marry me, Paige?"

"Yes," she said, throwing her arms around his wide shoulders. "I've never wanted anything more in my life than to be your wife."

"When? And please don't tell me you want a long engagement." He cupped her face with his palms. "We had more than ten years taken away from us, and I don't want to spend another minute without you."

"There's something I need to tell you," she said, knowing it was time to share her news with him. "I hope you're as happy about it as I am."

"What's that, sweetheart?" he asked, kissing her cheeks, her chin and the tip of her nose.

"You wasted your money the other day," she said, smiling.

He looked confused. "I'm not sure what you mean."

"At the pharmacy," she explained. "You bought a box of condoms because you'd read the journal entries and knew that Craig had purposely made me think I had a fertility problem."

Cole nodded. "I knew there was the chance that…" His voice trailed off, and she knew from the stunned look on his face that he had figured out what she was alluding to. "You're pregnant?"

"Yes."

"When did you find out?" he asked, glancing from her flat stomach to her face, then back to her stomach.

"I've been feeling kind of queasy the past few mornings and when I checked my calendar, I discovered that I was two weeks late," she said, loving the look of complete awe on his face. "I made a special trip to the pharmacy to get an in-home test this morning." She laughed. "I even took it twice with the same results."

"I know that having a baby on the way was the reason behind your marriage to Craig," Cole said, his expression turning serious. "And don't get me wrong, I'm happy about starting a family with you. But how do you feel about it?"

"Cole, I couldn't be happier about it," she said, touching his cheek. "I'm finally going to have a baby with the man I've loved for almost half of my life."

His wide grin thrilled her and she knew in her heart that her dreams were going to come true. She was going to marry the love of her life and finally have the family she'd always wanted. And he was as happy about all of it as she was.

A week later, standing in front of the fireplace in the family room, Cole handed Aaron the wedding band he would be slipping on Paige's finger. "Lose it and you're a dead man."

Aaron laughed as he slipped the ring into the pocket of his suit coat. "If I lose it, you'll have to be content with finishing off what's left of me after Stella gets done."

The pastor from one of the churches in Royal walked

over to stand on the other side of him, then Cole watched Stella enter the room and take her place on the other side of the minister. Looking toward the door leading out into the foyer, Paige stood there in a champagne-colored satin dress holding a bouquet of bright red roses and white daisies. Just the sight of her robbed him of breath and he knew it always would.

After they'd finally put the past to rest where it belonged, Cole had kept his word and spent every day since making sure that Paige knew just how much he cherished her. He had been given a second chance with the only woman he would ever love and he wasn't going to take that for granted.

As she walked across the room toward him, her loving smile sent a shaft of longing straight through him. "You're beautiful," he said when she stopped in front of him.

"And you, Mr. Richardson, are the most handsome man I've ever met," she said, her eyes reflecting a love that would last forever.

As they turned to face Reverend Holloway, Cole was glad that he and Paige had decided on a very small, intimate wedding with just Aaron and Stella for witnesses. A larger wedding would have taken a lot more planning and neither of them wanted to wait any longer than necessary to finally start their lives together.

In the week since he'd proposed, they had put a lot of plans into motion that both of them agreed would be the fresh start they wanted to get their marriage off on the right foot. The day he had taken Paige for a drive around the ranch, Cole had been scouting out the

best place to build a new house—one that was free of
ghosts from the past and unhappy memories. They'd
met with an architect yesterday, and they already had
the man drawing up plans for a new six-bedroom house
that included an in-home office for Cole to take care
of R&N business, as well as an art studio for Paige.

He and Aaron had also managed to hire several
more men, adding a couple of new work crews to the
new Royal office. With the additional help, they would
be able to keep up with the demands of their existing
contracts to rebuild the town, as well as build his and
Paige's new house. But the real winner was the Royal
economy. R&N Builders were helping to put people
back to work who had lost their jobs when the tornado
tore through the town.

The minister directed him to repeat his wedding
vows, and Cole turned to face his bride. "Paige, from
the moment I first saw you, I knew that we were meant
to be together—to share our lives and always be there
for each other. Your love makes me want to be a better
man and I give you my word that whatever life brings
our way, I will always love, honor and protect you."
He took the ring he'd handed Aaron earlier and gazing
into her eyes, slipped it on her finger. "With this ring,
I pledge myself to you for the rest of my life."

Tears filled her pretty gray eyes as she smiled up
at him. "Cole, you are my everything—my love, my
best friend and my partner in life. You have given me
more than I ever dreamed would be mine. In your eyes
I've finally found my home." Taking his wedding band
from Stella, Paige slid it onto his finger. "This ring is

a symbol of my never-ending love for you and I promise to honor and take care of you for all the days of my life."

He'd waited for years to hear her say those words. He knew this day and the days their children were born would be the happiest of his entire life.

"By the power vested in me by the great state of Texas, I now pronounce you husband and wife," Reverend Holloway said. The man smiled at Cole expectantly. "You can kiss your bride now, son."

"I love you, Paige Richardson," he said, unable to tell her enough how much she meant to him.

"And I love you, Cole Richardson." Her smile lit the darkest corners of his soul. "You are my heart and my soul for all of eternity."

Epilogue

Six months later

On the first anniversary of the tornado that had destroyed so much of the town and taken the lives of so many, Paige and Cole slowly made their way down Main Street toward the crowd gathering on the lawn of the newly finished Royal Town Hall. As they walked along hand in hand, Paige was pretty sure she resembled a duck.

Early on in her pregnancy the doctor had suspected she might be having twins, and a sonogram had confirmed that she and Cole were indeed having a little boy and a little girl. They both were thrilled by the news, but only two and a half months away from her due date, her belly was already big enough that she had started waddling when she walked.

"Do you need to sit down for a minute or two?" Cole asked as they strolled past Drew and Beth Farrell, who were laughing as they arranged pumpkins around the fall decorations they had donated for the day's ceremonies. Last year Beth's patch had been destroyed by the tornado, but this season it appeared to have produced a bumper crop. Pumpkins in all shapes and sizes, along with bales of straw and corn shocks, made a stunning fall display and reminded Paige that she and Cole needed to get one of the bigger pumpkins to carve for Halloween.

"Paige, are you all right?" Cole sounded worried that she hadn't answered his question.

Shaking her head, she smiled. "I'm fine. I can make it to the chairs in front of the podium. But I'd like to make a trip over to Beth's pumpkin patch within the next few days to get one for a jack-o'-lantern."

"Are you sure you're all right, sweetheart?" Cole asked, looking worried.

"Now look who's doing the fussing." She laughed.

He brought her hand up to kiss it. "You and our kids are my world, and I'm going to protect and take care of all of you."

"How are you feeling, Paige?" Megan Daltry asked as she and her husband, Whit, stopped to talk to them. A friend of Cole's and fellow Texas Cattleman's Club member, Whit owned Daltry Management Company and had helped Megan find her daughter, Evie, after the storm laid waste to the Little Tots Daycare. They'd been together ever since.

"I probably don't look like it, but I feel great," Paige said, patting her bulging stomach.

"Who is your doctor?" Megan asked. When Paige told her, Megan nodded. "That's who I'm going to."

"You're pregnant, too?" Paige hugged her friend. "I'm so happy for you."

"Yeah, we decided to give our daughter a little brother," Whit said, looking hopeful as he grinned from ear to ear. "But I'll be happy with a baby girl as long as she and Megan are all right."

"Congratulations!" Cole slapped Whit's shoulder in a friendly gesture. "We can attend Daddy Day Camp at Royal Memorial Hospital together."

"At least I'll have someone I know in that how-to workshop for new fathers," Whit said, looking relieved. "We can learn how to diaper a baby together."

"We'd better get to our seats," Cole said as the couple walked on ahead of them. "I don't want you having to stand throughout the ceremony."

"The Holts have arrived," Paige commented when she saw Lark and Keaton arrive with Skye and Jacob. Skye and Jacob had been having a rough time in their marriage when the tornado came through, but when Skye was injured Jacob had been there for her and during the time they spent together, they had worked through their problems. And Lark and Keaton had had to overcome a feud between their families. But after a rocky start for both couples, they had finally worked things out and couldn't be happier.

Both of the women were pregnant, and Paige couldn't help but wonder if the town was having its own little baby boom since the tornado had come through. It seemed that everywhere she looked there was another pregnant woman.

Watching Skye waddle after her baby daughter, Grace, Paige smiled. In a little more than a year, she would be chasing after her and Cole's babies as they toddled around. She had wanted to be able to do that for so long, she could hardly wait.

When Cole found them seats close to the stage that had been built for the memorial service to remember the lives lost in the tornado and the dedication ceremony of the new Town Hall, he helped her lower her bulk into the chair before sitting down beside her. "Are you comfortable, Paige?"

"You're fussing again, Mr. Richardson," she said, kissing his cheek.

"You're looking well, Paige," Julie Wakefield said as she and her husband Luc sat down in the seats next to her and Cole.

"I'm glad we got to see you," Luc told Cole. "Your company did a great job on rebuilding the hospital wing the tornado flattened and I'd like to see you and Aaron put in a bid from R&N Builders for the new wing Julie and I are planning to propose to the hospital board in a few weeks."

"It sounds to me like we'll be attending another dedication ceremony next year," Paige said, laughing.

Smiling, Julie nodded. "We hope so."

"Stella has been so good for Royal," Paige commented as the town's mayor stepped up to the podium. "After Richard Vance stepped down and Stella became the official mayor, she's done a wonderful job of bringing everyone together to rebuild the town. I don't think she'll have any trouble being re-elected."

Cole nodded. "She's also been the best thing that

ever happened to Aaron. He's more settled now than I've ever seen him."

When Stella read aloud the names of those killed during the storm and asked for a moment of silence, Cole reached down and took Paige's hand in his. Looking at each other, they silently acknowledged the loss of Craig, and she knew that, although he had done some terrible things to her and Cole, they both wished for him to rest in peace.

As Stella gave her speech and cut the ribbon for the official opening of the new town hall, the crowd was subdued, reflecting on their losses. But the applause that followed the ribbon cutting seemed to express hope for the future. When Stella was done, she paused for a moment as one of the city board members handed her a piece of paper.

"Is Dr. Marin in attendance today?" she asked, stepping back to the podium.

"I'm here," the doctor said, standing up a few chairs down from where Paige and Cole sat.

"You're going to be needed at the hospital very shortly," Stella said, smiling. "I've just been informed that Lark Holt is experiencing contractions and will be in need of your services."

As the ceremony wound down and the crowd began to disperse, Aaron approached his wife and handed their baby daughter to her before walking toward his car to get the diaper bag.

Paige and Cole laughed as they thought of how panicked Aaron had been when Stella had gone into labor. The look on his face had been priceless.

"You know you shouldn't laugh," Paige told Cole as he helped her up from the chair. "You'll be wearing the same expression and taking me on a wild car ride in about three months."

Cole wrapped his arms around her and gave her a kiss that made her legs feel weak and shaky. Then tucking her to his side as they walked toward their car, he said, "Sweetheart, I'll be glad to give you as many wild rides as you want."

Paige looked at the man she loved with all of her heart and soul. Cole was a loving husband and he was going to be a wonderful father. Sometimes she had to pinch herself in order to believe it was all real.

"Are you happy, Cole?" she asked when he helped her into the passenger seat of the car.

"I can honestly say the past six months have been the happiest of my life, Paige," he said, leaning down to give her a tender kiss. After closing her door, he walked around the car to slide into the driver's seat and start the engine. "Now let's go home so I can fuss over you some more."

"Have I told you lately how much I love you?" she asked.

Laughing, he nodded. "Yeah, but I never get tired of hearing it."

"I love you, Cole."

"And I love you, Paige. Now and until the end of time."

* * * * *

TEXAS CATTLEMAN'S CLUB:
AFTER THE STORM
Don't miss a single story!

STRANDED WITH THE RANCHER
by Janice Maynard

SHELTERED BY THE MILLIONAIRE
by Catherine Mann

PREGNANT BY THE TEXAN
by Sara Orwig

BECAUSE OF THE BABY...
by Cat Schield

HIS LOST AND FOUND FAMILY
by Sarah M. Anderson

MORE THAN A CONVENIENT BRIDE
by Michelle Celmer

FOR HIS BROTHER'S WIFE
by Kathie Denosky

If you're on Twitter, tell us what you think of
Harlequin Desire! #harlequindesire

COMING NEXT MONTH FROM

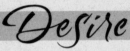

HARLEQUIN
Desire
™

Available May 5, 2015

#2371 TRIPLE THE FUN
Billionaires and Babies • by Maureen Child
Nothing will stand between Connor and his triplets, not even their stubborn, sexy guardian. But Dina wants to raise the babies on her terms, even if it means resisting the most domineering—and desirable—man she's ever met.

#2372 MINDING HER BOSS'S BUSINESS
Dynasties: The Montoros • by Janice Maynard
Alex is on a royal mission for his country's throne. But when his assistant cozies up to a prince, unexpected jealously forces Alex to reevaluate his ideas about separating work from play...

#2373 KISSED BY A RANCHER
Lone Star Legends • by Sara Orwig
Josh seeks shelter at Abby's B&B...and gets snowed in! When they share a moonlit kiss, legend says it will lead to love. But can a cautious, small-town girl and a worldly Texas rancher turn myth into real romance?

#2374 THE SHEIKH'S PREGNANCY PROPOSAL
by Fiona Brand
After risking one passionate night with a sheikh, Sarah dismisses her dreams for a relationship—until her lover finds out she's pregnant. Suddenly, the rules change, because Gabe *must* marry the mother of his child!

#2375 SECRET HEIRESS, SECRET BABY
At Cain's Command • by Emily McKay
When Texas tycoon Grant Shepard seduced the lost Cain heiress, he ultimately walked away to protect her from her conniving family. But now she's back...and with a little secret that changes everything.

#2376 SEX, LIES AND THE CEO
Chicago Sons • by Barbara Dunlop
To prove the Colborns stole her late father's invention, Darci Rivers goes undercover at Colborn Aerospace—and even starts dating her billionaire boss! Can a double deception lead to an honest shot at happiness?

YOU CAN FIND MORE INFORMATION ON UPCOMING HARLEQUIN® TITLES, FREE EXCERPTS AND MORE AT WWW.HARLEQUIN.COM.

HDCNM0415

REQUEST YOUR FREE BOOKS!
2 FREE NOVELS PLUS 2 FREE GIFTS!

HARLEQUIN®

Desire

ALWAYS POWERFUL, PASSIONATE AND PROVOCATIVE

YES! Please send me 2 FREE Harlequin Desire® novels and my 2 FREE gifts (gifts are worth about $10). After receiving them, if I don't wish to receive any more books, I can return the shipping statement marked "cancel." If I don't cancel, I will receive 6 brand-new novels every month and be billed just $4.55 per book in the U.S. or $4.99 per book in Canada. That's a savings of at least 13% off the cover price! It's quite a bargain! Shipping and handling is just 50¢ per book in the U.S. and 75¢ per book in Canada.* I understand that accepting the 2 free books and gifts places me under no obligation to buy anything. I can always return a shipment and cancel at any time. Even if I never buy another book, the two free books and gifts are mine to keep forever.

225/326 HDN F4ZC

Name _____ (PLEASE PRINT)

Address _____ Apt. #

City _____ State/Prov. _____ Zip/Postal Code

Signature (if under 18, a parent or guardian must sign)

Mail to the **Harlequin® Reader Service:**
IN U.S.A.: P.O. Box 1867, Buffalo, NY 14240-1867
IN CANADA: P.O. Box 609, Fort Erie, Ontario L2A 5X3

Want to try two free books from another line?
Call 1-800-873-8635 or visit www.ReaderService.com.

* Terms and prices subject to change without notice. Prices do not include applicable taxes. Sales tax applicable in N.Y. Canadian residents will be charged applicable taxes. Offer not valid in Quebec. This offer is limited to one order per household. Not valid for current subscribers to Harlequin Desire books. All orders subject to credit approval. Credit or debit balances in a customer's account(s) may be offset by any other outstanding balance owed by or to the customer. Please allow 4 to 6 weeks for delivery. Offer available while quantities last.

Your Privacy—The Harlequin® Reader Service is committed to protecting your privacy. Our Privacy Policy is available online at www.ReaderService.com or upon request from the Harlequin Reader Service.

We make a portion of our mailing list available to reputable third parties that offer products we believe may interest you. If you prefer that we not exchange your name with third parties, or if you wish to clarify or modify your communication preferences, please visit us at www.ReaderService.com/consumerchoice or write to us at Harlequin Reader Service Preference Service, P.O. Box 9062, Buffalo, NY 14269. Include your complete name and address.

HDI3R

SPECIAL EXCERPT FROM

HARLEQUIN

Desire

*Alex Ramon is all business when he's tasked with
restoring his country's royal family to the throne.
But when his sexy assistant cozies up to a prince,
his unexpected jealousy requires him to mix work
with pleasure…*

Read on for a sneak peek at
MINDING HER BOSS'S BUSINESS
the passionate first installment in the
DYNASTIES: THE MONTOROS *series!*

When a small orchestra launched into their first song,
Alex stood and held out his hand. "Do you feel like
dancing?"

He knew it was a tactical error as soon as he took
Maria in his arms. Given the situation, he'd assumed
dancing was a socially acceptable way to pass the time.

He was wrong. Dead wrong. No matter the public
venue or the circumspect way in which he held her, nothing could erase the fact that Maria was soft and warm in
his embrace. The slick fabric of her dress did nothing to
disguise the skin beneath.

He found his breath caught in his throat, lodged there
by a sharp stab of hunger. He'd worked so hard these past
weeks he'd let his personal needs slide. Celibacy was
neither smart nor sustainable. Certainly not when faced
daily with such deliciously carnal temptation.

When he couldn't think of a good reason to let her

go, one dance turned into three. Inevitably, his body responded to her nearness.

He was in heaven and hell, shuddering with arousal and unable to do a thing about it.

When the potential future prince brushed past them, his petite sister in his arms, Alex remembered what he had meant to say earlier. "Maria…"

"Hmm?"

Her voice had the warm, honeyed sound of a woman pleasured by her lover. Alex cleared his throat. "You need to be careful around Gabriel Montoro."

Maria's reaction was unmistakable. She went rigid and pulled away. "Excuse me?" Beautiful eyes glared at him.

Alex soldiered on. "He's a mature, experienced man, and you are very young. I'd hate to see him take advantage of you."

Maria went pale but for two spots of hectic color on her cheekbones. "Your concern is duly noted," she said, the words icy. "But you'll have to trust my judgment, I'm afraid."

Find out if Alex heeds Maria's advice (hint: he doesn't!)
in MINDING HER BOSS'S BUSINESS
by USA TODAY bestselling author
Janice Maynard.
Available May 2015 wherever
Harlequin Desire books and ebooks are sold

www.Harlequin.com

Copyright © 2015 by Janice Maynard

HDEXP0415

Love the Harlequin book you just read?

Your opinion matters.

Review this book on your favorite book site, review site, blog or your own social media properties and share your opinion with other readers!

Be sure to connect with us at:
Harlequin.com/Newsletters
Facebook.com/HarlequinBooks
Twitter.com/HarlequinBooks

HREVIEWS

JUST CAN'T GET ENOUGH?

Join our social communities
and talk to us online.

You will have access to the latest
news on upcoming titles and special
promotions, but most importantly,
you can talk to other fans about your
favorite Harlequin reads.

Harlequin.com/Community

 Facebook.com/HarlequinBooks

 Twitter.com/HarlequinBooks

Pinterest.com/HarlequinBooks

THE WORLD IS BETTER WITH

Romance

Harlequin has everything from contemporary, passionate and heartwarming to suspenseful and inspirational stories.

Whatever your mood, we have a romance just for you!

Connect with us to find your next great read, special offers and more.

 /HarlequinBooks

@HarlequinBooks

www.HarlequinBlog.com

www.Harlequin.com/Newsletters

HARLEQUIN®

A *Romance* FOR EVERY MOOD™

www.Harlequin.com

SERIESHALOAD2015